RELENTLESS:
THE SEARCH FOR
TYPHOID MARY
Abridged Edition

A Novel

Based on the true story

by

Joan Meijer

Published by:

JEM Publishing
2851 West Avenue L #196
Lancaster, CA 93536

joanmeijer@gmail.com

© 2013 by Joan E. Meijer. All rights Reserved
ISBN: 978-1-931191-29-6

This story is a novel based on the true story of Mary Mallon. Although the facts of the story are real, the characters and dialogue are fictional. They were inspired by the history as reported by George Soper in his published speeches and articles and other documents of the time.

Also available in Audio and on Kindle and other Digital Readers

Dedicated to my mother Bonnie Prudden an amazing act to follow.

Bonnie Prudden was truly an original woman who changed the world around her. One of the best and most recognized rock climbers of her day – man or woman and featured in the documentary *Up Rope* and more recent books and documentaries as well. The first woman nominated to the National Ski Patrol for her work in pre-ski exercises. The first woman on the cover of *Sports Illustrated* (not in a bathing suit). Author of 33 books – including the best selling *How To Keep Slender And Fit After 30* and *Pain Erasure*. The first fitness expert on National Television appearing weekly on *Dave Garraway's The Today Show*. A founding member of *The President's Council on Youth Fitness* (now *The President's Council on Physical Fitness and Nutrition*) which was founded by President Eisenhower largely because of her major study on youth fitness. A pioneer in infant swimming. In her later years she greatly advanced the pain relief therapy myotheray and probably did a dozen things I've forgotten. She inspired me in so many ways, by telling me early:

"All of us have been put on this earth to make a difference. Find out what it is you love and give it all you've got."

That's how she lived her life – and that's how I'm trying to live mine.

Acknowledgements

I want to thank my grandparents Gula V Hirschland and Franz H. Hirschland for introducing me to the kind of wealthy household in which Mary cooked so that I would know first hand what her life was like. I also want to thank the original Aggie, Agnes McCarthy, who was their maid and ours and who helped raise my sister and me at an important time in our lives. Aggie introduced me to the Irish brogue and tuneless song that lives in my head to this day. I want to thank my daughter Jacky, her husband Michael and my grandson Lance for putting up with me when I'm writing. I also want to thank my sister Suzy Prudden who makes all things possible and is one of my greatest support systems. I want to thank Bill Rapp for insisting that I turn into the writer I have become.

If it's possible I want to thank the accident of the family into which I was born. I was fortunate enough to live in a New York that was on the cusp of change. I lived in a railroad tenement on Second Avenue and thought it rather campy without realizing its history. I spent as much time as possible with my grandparents in their mansion in Westchester County New York without really realizing they were privileged. I was fortunate enough to skirt the edges of the places Mary lived and understood both of the cultures in which she functioned because they were part of my own life.

RELENTLESS: THE SEARCH FOR TYPHOID MARY

Part I – Discovery

Chapter 1

Peach Ice Cream

Who could ever have foreseen that the George Townsend House would be the epicenter for the solution of one of the world's great medical mysteries? That house, located near the southern tip of Long Island in Oyster Bay, New York was, for want of a better description, gracious. From its large central chimney with four distinct flues – that guaranteed heat throughout the cold, damp winters – to its multiple steeply slanting roofs, expansive porches, sloping lawns and ancient trees, it spoke of wealth, comfort and grace at a glance. Built in 1885, it combined a first story of red brick and second and third stories of wood that had been painted a rich enamel gray. Striped canvas awnings extended the porches, providing shade during the hot, muggy summer months.

A long drive curled up the hill from Prospect Street at the top of which the house sat like the featured piece in a Victorian novel. The drive rounded the barn that had once provided shelter for carriages and horses and now served as a garage for the horseless carriages that more and more were the transportation of choice for the wealthy tenants who summered at the house. Maple, oak and linden trees lined the drive and sheltered the house from the worst of the muggy summer heat. From the house Oyster Bay Harbor itself could be seen and beyond the bay Long Island Sound glittered in the brilliant sunshine.

The occupants of the house could walk to the beach, followed by their servants carrying picnic baskets, blankets, towels and the umbrellas that sheltered them from the relentless summer sun. The house was perfectly positioned for New York's wealthy seeking escape from the cholera-riddled city in the summer months.

The Townsend House kitchen was large and white. Its floors were covered with linoleum tiles. Linoleum, which had been invented in 1860, was considered a state of the art floor covering. The installation of this revolutionary floor covering made the house even more attractive to the wealthy summer tenants. The tiles were white – like the kitchen – and inlaid with a popular pattern of small black squares at each of the corners of the larger squares which had been set side by side and end to end.

There were two large sinks in the kitchen, one for washing vegetables and one for washing dishes. Between the two sinks were wooden areas, slanted for draining. The stove was coal burning and large enough for a restaurant. It radiated heat that made the kitchen almost unbearable during the heat waves of summer. In the center of the kitchen was a large cutting table made of gray marble slab. Cabinets for dried and canned foods, herbs and spices, lined the wall opposite the sinks. A small room off the kitchen contained stacks of pots, pans, coffee grinders and general cooking equipment in sufficient numbers to prepare parties for up to 100.

At the far end of the kitchen, away from the working end, was a long table for a staff of between six and twelve. Dishes and cutlery for the staff were kept in tall cabinets that lined the far wall. Dishes for the family and guests were kept in the pantry, a room between the kitchen and the dining area. The pantry had its own sink and access to such luxuries as butterball paddles, melon scoops and the crystal dishes in which fresh celery and olives were served.

Off the pantry was a cutting room with its own door leading to the outside of the house. In the cutting room Onofrio, the gardener, would leave buckets of fresh cut flowers for the mistress of the house to arrange in a collection of vases. Fresh flowers were regularly distributed throughout the house by the various maids who oversaw the different areas. Onofrio also left baskets of fresh vegetables from the gardens for the cook which, because the room had its own entrance, he could do without tracking mud into the kitchen.

A long passage that led to the laundry room at the end of the house completed the servant's area of the house. The laundry had been placed at a distance from the kitchen because its steaming vats of simmering starch in combination with its giant, steam driven mangles created their own heat and, in combination with the cast iron coal stove in the kitchen, would have driven the staff to insurrection during the dog days of summer.

Across the hall from the laundry was the servant's toilet, which had taken the place of a very small closet, once used for coats in winter. The fact that the Townsend House boasted indoor plumbing had been the selling point for the Charles Henry Warren family, which had rented the house for the summer. Doris Warren had been adamant. She insisted that she would never again rent a house in which she would be subjected to the foul odors and inconvenience of an outhouse, even if the family privy was separate from the one used by the help. The General, a banker who could afford to cosset his much adored bride of ten years – as he liked to refer to her – had been delighted to indulge her with the gift of the Townsend House. It was a perfect summer establishment, close enough to the city –

in case business required his attendance in the office – far enough away to provide a haven for his wife and children.

The crowning glory of the house was its proximity to Sagamore Hill, the summer White House of Theodore Roosevelt, 26th President of the United States, and his family. The General and his wife were invited to dine with the Roosevelts on occasion, as were other well-positioned families in the area.

On this day in early August, Mary Mallon, who had recently been hired to replace the Warren's regular cook – who had inconveniently developed appendicitis and was recovering from complications of surgery – was preparing her signature dish of peach ice cream, designed to justify Mrs. Warren's choice of her as a summer replacement. Mary believed that half of her sterling recommendations were the result of peach ice cream. To cement her position in the household even more firmly, Mary had invited the two Warren children to help in the preparation of this much admired rarity. Mary had discovered – during her years as a cook for the wealthiest families of New York – that the sure path to acceptance lay in the children.

She was, in fact, a rather intimidating woman; tall, broad in her body, extremely strong and apt to move more like a man than a woman in a society that prized the simpering steps of femininity. Her only attractive features were her eyes, crystal blue and shining with intelligence.

Set out on the table was an ice cream machine comprised of a bucket with a large bowl in it that could be turned with a crank. A smaller bowl of peeled and sliced peaches sat waiting to be mashed in the ice cream machine's inner bowl together with four large brown eggs. The wire potato masher, which would be used for mashing and mixing, rested beside the eggs.

The children's wide eyes followed Mary as she carried the ice cream machine's bucket to the vegetable sink where a large block of ice could be seen glistening in the warm summer air. They stared in awe as she took an ice pick in her large, strong hand and attacked the block, stabbing at it so that chips, large and small, flew into the sink around it. Twice she stopped chipping and handed a small wedge of ice to each of the children to suck on as a treat. When she judged there were enough chips, she stopped the attack on the ice, and scooped up the frozen water with her hands and dumped the chips into the bucket.

"Is it the ice that turns the cream to ice cream, Mary?" Abigail asked her voice breathless with awe.

"Of course it is, that's why they call it 'ice cream,' silly bean," Constance informed her younger sibling. Constance was at an age where she knew everything and her voice was thick with superiority. Abigail made a face as if to say that she had only been making conversation. If she had dared stick out her tongue she would have. Constance regularly used her two years seniority to great advantage with Abigail much to her younger sister's great consternation.

"Mind you, you don't add the ice to the cream. You just cool the cream with the ice until it thickens in a certain way," Mary instructed, ignoring the atmosphere of disagreement between the two children. "It's quite a miracle. Without the ice it would just turn to whipped cream or butter."

"Where did the ice come from?" Abigail asked.

"Well now, there's a great ice house on the grounds. I suppose they'll be bringin' the blocks in from some big river, like the Hudson, durin' the winter. They store it in straw and then use it all through the summer for cold drinks and the like. It's a great luxury," Mary's strong Irish brogue and Gaelic rhythms punctuated her speech like a song.

"We almost never have it," Constance mused, her voice dreamy with expectation of the treat.

Mary smiled knowingly as she drew the bowl with the peaches toward her and picked up the potato masher. "There's undoubtedly a very good reason why the good Lord made the things that taste the best, take the longest to prepare. Perhaps so we wouldn't ever be tempted to forget that we're eatin' somethin' special.

"Would you like to take turns mashin' the peaches?" she asked, as she demonstrated the way to mash the fruit. Both children nodded enthusiastically. Mary handed the bowl and masher to Constance, "You first Miss Constance."

It was at this moment that Doris Warren, in her soft flowing white-flowered gown with its Lego' mutton sleeves, pinched waist and high bustle chose to make her appearance in the kitchen. The antithesis of Mary, Mr. Warren's bride wore her soft brown hair piled high with gentle ringlets cascading down her narrow back. She was a walking statement of the hours it took to scrub her grass stained hems, lace her into her breath restricting corsets and coif her ringlets to perfection.

"Don't let the children bother you Mary," she drawled, her perfect English spoken with the clenched jaw that symbolized all the restrictions of the upper class.

"Children never bother me, Mrs. Warren. I've a spot for them and that's a fact," Mary smiled. She stood almost a foot taller and at least that much wider than the diminutive Doris Warren and might have seemed threatening in other circumstances.

"Do you have children of your own?" asked the ever-inquisitive Abigail.

"I had a daughter, once." Mary replied, a cloud dimming the brilliance of her startlingly blue eyes.

"Where is your daughter now?" Abigail asked.

"Miss Abigail, are you big enough to go to the ice chest and get the pitcher of cream all by yourself?" Mary asked, diverting the child from what threatened to become an uncomfortable conversation.

"Oh yes. Thank you, Mary," Abigail said, dimpling with happiness.

"Where is your daughter Mary?" Constance pursued, not satisfied with the change of subject.

"Constance," Doris chided. "Prying into other people's personal lives is bad manners."

"I was just..."

Doris fixed her with an angry stare and Constance backed down.

"I'll be needin' the sugar jar, Miss Constance," Mary said after enough time had passed so that it wouldn't appear as if she was undermining her employer. "Would you be able to be findin' it for me?"

"I know just where it is, Mary," Constance replied, putting down the potato masher and dashing off to the shelf where the sugar jar was stored.

"If they get to be too much Mary, just send them to Nanny. Though I must say, she's appreciative for a little time to herself now that you're here," Doris Warren said, taking advantage of the girl's absence. "We're so grateful that you could come to help us on such short notice."

"It's my pleasure Mrs. Warren," Mary replied.

They were able to exchange only those few words before the girls returned, racing each other to be the first to bring the treasures they had been sent to find.

"Don't bump your sister, Constance," Doris Warren scolded.

Constance deflected the reprimand by instigating a happy chant, "We're making ice-cream, we're making ice-cream..."

"This is such a treat for them. Thank you for letting them help, Mary," Doris said gazing at her oldest daughter with a knowing eye.

"I enjoy havin' 'em in the kitchen and that's a fact," Mary replied, her horsey face splitting into a wide grin. "Thank you Miss Constance. Now I'll be needin' the measuring cups. Miss Abigail. Good girl, you didn't spill a drop."

"I was very careful," Abigail said, pride filling her voice.

"So I see. Would you like to have a turn mashin' the peaches now?" Mary asked.

"Oh, yes please," Abigail said happily.

"Here are the measuring cups," Constance announced dragging attention back to herself.

"Thank you, Miss Constance."

The girls settled down to taking turns with the masher.

Minutes passed until Mary said, "That's fine now, Miss Abigail. Let's be settin' the peaches on the ice." Mary took the bowl and the potato masher from Abigail, banged the masher against the rim of the bowl to rid it of any remaining chunks of peach, and placed the bowl in the bucket of ice. "Miss Constance would you be wantin' to measure half a cup a sugar and pour it over the peaches while I separate the eggs?"

"Yes please," Constance said. She carefully poured the sugar until it reached the top of the half cup, then transferred it slowly to the peaches.

Meanwhile, Mary removed the eggs from the bowl, cracked one, pried it into two halves and, tipped the yolk back and forth between the shells allowing the white to slide into an empty bowl she had set aside for that purpose. When the yolk was free of white, she dumped them onto the peaches. She repeated this process three more times to the wide-eyed approval of both children.

"This is called separatin' the eggs," she explained. "We'll just keep the whites separate and I'll make you a meringue to eat with the ice cream later on. The recipe calls for yolks only."

"Can we help with the meringue too?" Abigail asked.

"We'll see if you want to after all the stirrin' you're going to do. Meringue takes a great deal of stirrin' and beatin' as well. Now Miss Abigail, please pour the cream over the peaches," Mary instructed. "Miss Constance you may take this fork and pop the egg yolks."

When the cream had been added and the egg yolks popped, Mary fitted the lid of the ice cream machine in place and then clamped the bucket to the side of the table.

"Now, let's see who is goin' to turn first? Miss Abigail I think it will be you because Miss Constance was the first to mash the peaches. You'll turn twenty times and then it will be Miss Constance's turn." Constance opened her mouth as if to protest. "Now don't' be frettin', Miss Constance. You'll each have so many turns at the crank before we're through you'll never be wantin' to make ice cream again."

"I'll want to make ice cream every day," Abigail smiled as she pushed against the crank.

It was difficult at first because the ice had hardened against the bowl. Mary had to help Abigail get started but once the bowl was spinning the crank moved easily and the child had no trouble turning it.

"One, two, three... Keep it turnin' Miss Abigail; you don't want to let it rest. If you let the cream rest, it might turn into somethin' all together different from what you expected."

"Like what?" Abigail asked, laughter coloring her voice.

"Oh, like liquorice stew, or hot cross buns," Mary smiled.

"No it wouldn't," Constance said derisively.

"Twelve, thirteen... Keep turnin', Miss Abigail. That's a girl," Mary said.

Doris Warren slipped out of the kitchen and let herself into the flower room where fresh cut flowers and greens stood in buckets waiting for her to arrange them. She smiled happily as she busied herself with a chore she truly enjoyed. The joyful sounds of her children added to her satisfaction. It was truly a memorable afternoon.

Chapter 2

The Wonderful Summer

Summer passed with a joyful similarity of days. Although there were a sufficient number of marvelous moments to last them through the dark and cold of winter, the spectacular evening of the peach ice cream was outstanding in everyone's mind.

"We helped cook it," Abigail announced to her father, pride reflected in every part of her being.

"And we helped make the meringue even though Mary didn't think we would want to after we cooked the ice cream for so long," Constance added.

"I didn't know you cook ice cream," General Warren mused, delighting in the girls' pride and excitement.

"Well, you don't really. You put it in ice and you stir it for ages until it gets thick. Mary says that if you only let the cream sit in the ice, without stirring it all the time, it will become liquorice stew but I don't believe her," Abigail giggled.

The children watched with high concern as the General dipped his spoon into the pale dessert with its flecks of peach. They didn't relax until he groaned with pleasure.

"This is the best dessert I have ever tasted in my entire life," he announced. And with that, Doris and the children dug into their own delicious mounds exclaiming, with deepest satisfaction, pure enjoyment of the miracle that had been created out of mashed peaches, cream, sugar and ice.

For the rest if their time in Oyster Bay the family stuck to a fairly rigid routine. The General felt that routine had a stabilizing influence on the girls and insisted that the days be scheduled even if they were on vacation. Each morning at precisely ten, the family strolled along the sidewalk that wound through the village, children in tow. Doris delighted in showing off her flowing morning finery. Every day she sported new and magnificent hats bearing fruits and feathers to match the colors of the acres of material that had gone into her gowns and matching parasols as befitted the wife of one of New York's important bankers.

The General – who sported a fashionable handlebar moustache – wore his cutaway morning coat, with a high-buttoned waistcoat over a high-collared shirt all this above his creased fly-front trousers and highly polished leather boots. As they walked, the General tipped his top hat in formal greeting to the other males of his class who took their morning constitutionals with their own families. They were trailed by servants who would carry whatever shopping Doris might be inclined to do. For her part, she laced her gloved hand through the General's arm and held her parasol against the summer sun to protect her delicate skin.

On occasion they stopped in the park that surrounded the Derby-Hall Bandstand so that the children could meet and play with summer friends, some of whom they already knew from the City. The girls played on the swings, the merry-go-round, slides and seesaws. They engaged in endless games of tag, skipped rope and chased hoops that the servants had brought with them. While the children played under the watchful eyes of their nannies, the parents sipped tea at the soda fountain at nearby Snouders Drug Store – the only place in all of Oyster Bay that boasted a telephone. Even President Roosevelt did not have a telephone, either at the Summer White House at Saganaw Hill or at his offices on the second floor of Moore House. Snouder's son Arthur had the important task of delivering messages from Washington whenever they arrived. Because of the phone, Snouder's was the most frequented gathering place for the summer businessmen and their wives. While the women gossiped about the new fashions from Paris, the men discussed whatever news had filtered in from the City via the *Oyster Bay Guardian* or the day-old *New York Times*.

In the afternoons, the family went bathing together at the nearby beach. In their bathing costumes and robes they marched down the hill to the bay, once again followed by several servants carrying an incredible amount of paraphernalia required for bathing as they called it. Doris and the girls wore black, knee-length, wool bathing dresses with puffed sleeves each of which featured a white trimmed sailor collar. The dresses were worn over bloomers trimmed with ribbons and bows which in turn were worn over long black stockings and lace-up bathing slippers. The outfits were topped off with fancy mop caps to protect their hair. Doris carried a parasol to protect her skin even when cooling herself in the water. Pale skin was the mark of her class and she valued it as much as she valued her clothing.

The General was covered in black wool as well. His outfit was more along the lines of a long sleeve T-shirt and tights that ended in stockings and his own bathing slippers. The family was grateful for the calm waters of the bay which allowed them to enjoy the cool water without the threat of being knocked over by waves or pulled under by their clothing. The Atlantic side of Long Island with its constant waves was considered too rough for the women.

While the servants set up chairs and umbrellas and put out snacks for the children, the family watched the local people who came out to the beaches to dig for clams. Like most of the summer visitors, the Warrens were particularly intrigued by the weather-beaten Indian woman who lived in a tiny cabin on the beach. It was from her that the Warrens bought a bucket of clams in the middle of July for a magnificent feast of steamed clams and whenever they saw her they talked about having clams again before they departed for the city at the end of August.

"I don't like clams," Constance insisted, arranging her face in a scowl that indicated a battle over dinner.

"Don't worry darling, I promised you that we wouldn't eat them raw ever again. We'll give them to Mary and she will make us clams that you will love almost as much as you enjoyed the oyster stew we had in July," Doris soothed, trying to keep the laughter off her face as she remembered the first and only time Constance had tried raw clams.

"I don't like steamed clams either," Constance said, stamping her foot.

"Well then Mary will make you something you do like. Mommy and Daddy will eat the clams and you can eat them when you're older and have a more refined taste," Doris replied, ignoring the look on Constance's face that bespoke a wrestling match between her assumed dislike of clams and her desire to be old enough to eat them.

"I like clams," Abigail piped in, sealing the argument for Constance. She would eat the clams even if they made her sick.

But they never did get around to buying them, although in late August Doris had planned to have company over for that clam dinner and had asked the General whether to invite the Morris family as well as the Sinclaires over to join them.

Most evenings the family would play 20-Questions and sing popular songs around the spinet that Doris Warren played so well. They read poetry, taking turns guessing the poet, or simply listened to Doris Warren read from the books they found at the People's Library and Reading Room on East Main Street.

As she read, the children drew pictures or cut out clothing for paper dolls. On Sundays they attended the Christ Church of Oyster Bay which was the house of worship that the Roosevelts also attended.

Mary and the rest of the staff went to services at St. Dominic's Church and Chapel, which boasted a magnificent original pipe organ that was the pride of the congregation. It was an American made Hook and Hastings Opus Tracker organ. The congregation boasted that it was one of only three of its kind in all of America. But, although the staff was inordinately proud of the church pipe organ, they never mentioned its existence inside the house fearing that the family might take exception to their conceit.

On a sunny Saturday, two weeks before they were scheduled to return to New York to take up their winter lives, the Warren family gathered for a professional photograph on the front porch of the large house. Doris was dressed in her finest lavender gingham gown, a hat with orioles and cherries perched atop her pile of curled hair and a lavender parasol. The children wore matching frocks with large lace trimmed collars, and the General was in his finest black suit with his high starched collar, his black high top perched at an angle atop his head, his handlebar moustache carefully waxed into quarter-size curls.

The photographer brought a large box camera which he set up on a tripod. The family was assembled. Doris sat in a rocker with Abigail on her knee and Constance standing beside her. The General posed just behind all of them smiling his contentment. The photographer pulled a dark cloth over his head and the view finder. He held a tray of flash powder high in the air to light the scene for the photograph. When the picture was properly centered, he squeezed the bulb that set off the flash powder and simultaneously took the photograph. This process was repeated numerous times to assure that the family had at least one perfect picture as a memory of their perfect summer.

It was the night of August 27th that typhoid struck Constance. By September 3rd it had taken Onofrio, Irene –

the downstairs maid, Tom – the footman, Hatti – the laundress, Abigail and finally the exhausted Doris – who had spent the early part of the week nursing her children.

Mary knew exactly what to do. She had seen typhoid more times than she cared to remember. Most of the time it just made people sick in varying degrees. Sometimes it was fatal. She knew that she should bathe the children in tepid water to keep their fevers down. She knew that she should make them drink cool water to keep them hydrated. She knew enough to watch those who were not yet sick carefully to make certain that they were cared for early in the development of the disease. She hurried from patient to patient bringing them water and sponging their pain wracked bodies.

On the night that Doris contracted the disease she had been nursing Abigail and Constance who were lying in separate beds both deathly ill. Doris had relieved Mary of the task of sponging Constance so that she could attend to the members of the staff who had been stricken. Without warning blood seeped from Doris' nose. Without realizing that she was bleeding, she wiped the viscous fluid, smearing the blood across her face. At that moment Mary came into the room carrying a fresh pitcher of ice water

"Here we are, Mrs. Warren. We'll just get a little more fluid in them. It's good for bringin' down the fe--. Oh look, she's got the rose spots on her belly. She'll be all right now," Mary said, turning and looking at Doris for the first time. "Oh, dear God, Mrs. Warren, you'd better come and lie down."

"I'm fine, Mary," Doris Warren said, her voice reflecting the exhaustion she felt.

"No you're not, Mrs. Warren. You're as sick as your daughters. And if you don't lie down you might even die. I know this sickness. You have to respect it, or certainly it will do you in." Doris did not protest as Mary helped her to her feet and half carried her to her bedroom.

"Come along now, Mrs. Warren. I'll take care of the little ones, never you worry. I'm very good at this. I've had a lot of practice," Mary said, reassuring Doris Warren even as she took control of the household.

When they reached the Warren bedroom, Doris swayed on her feet, seemingly unable to figure out what to do next.

"Will ya' be wantin' some help with getting in your night clothes, Mrs. Warren?" Mary asked, pouring some water into the bowl on the night stand, rinsing off a rag and cleaning Doris Warren's face.

"What's the matter, Mary?" the General asked from the doorway. He had heard Mary's voice in the hallway and hurried upstairs to see what was happening.

"Mrs. Warren has become sick, General," Mary said through tightly compressed lips. "Do you mind if I help her change into her night clothes?"

"No, I'd be grateful. Is there something I can do to help?" the General asked.

"You'd best be protectin' yourself General," Mary said.

"I've had typhoid," the General replied. "I won't get it again."

"Well then, I brought some water up for the children," Mary replied. "If you'd encourage 'em to drink a glass that would be good for them. I'll call you when I have gotten Mrs. Warren in bed. We'll be needin' to get her to drink water too."

It was a terrible time. Mary lovingly cared for the children, nursed Doris Warren, cared for Onofrio, Irene, Tom and Hatti. Mrs. Townsend, the owner of the house, came to supervise the care of Onofrio – who, for several days stood at death's door. In those intense days Mary did not sleep in her bed once. When she was not sponging, spoon feeding or cleaning up after her patients, she sat in a chair in the children's room soothing and comforting them.

She was there as Abigail began to show the signs of having turned the corner developing her own rosy rash that proclaimed the turning point of the infection. But even on the road to recovery the children remained very sick.

Toward the last days of their illness Mary hardly dared to sit, so profound was her exhaustion. She was afraid that she would fall asleep and miss a moment when the children needed her. But on the morning that Abigail finally awoke from her fevered torpor Mary had succumbed to her exhaustion and sat snoring in her rocking chair.

"Mary?" Abigail said her small child's voice filled at the wonder of finding Mary asleep in the chair.

"Good mornin', darlin'. You're feeling better I see," Mary said, squinting at the child through eyes that still burned with exhaustion.

"I'm hungry," Abigail announced.

"Me too, Mary," Constance joined in, awakening at the sound of her sister's voice.

"I'll make you some eggs," Mary said, smiling at the certainty that the children were now on the road to recovery.

"And bacon," Abigail said.

"And bacon," Mary replied.

Chapter 3

Without Cause

It was the kind of wet, cold and windy winter day that chilled New Yorkers to the bone. The streets of lower Manhattan were crowded and treacherous. Unmelted slush mixed with the filth of hundreds of horses that pulled the carts and carriages that kept the city's commerce alive. The mixture had covered the roads with a slippery brown mush with an underpinning of ice where water had pooled during a recent warm spell.

The street was crowded with people on foot competing for space with carriages, trolleys and carts. Occasionally backfiring – from the impurities of the gas that fueled an increasing number of automobiles – caused a ruckus with the horses when they passed through. The backfires exploded like gun shots with magnified echoes as the sound ricocheted against the brick buildings that lined each street.

Esther Townsend, a genteel, slender, dignified septuagenarian, as dry and wrinkled as an old apple doll, dressed in fur-trimmed black, picked her way across the street after debarking from a Hansom Cab. Her objective was a massive brick structure which pronounced itself "The New York Department of Health" in gold leaf above the door.

On entering, she stamped the collection of snow and horse droppings that marred her laced leather boots and walked purposefully to the section of the wall marked "Office Directory". George Soper, Ph.D.'s office was listed on the fifth floor. Esther Townsend eyed the new fangled Otis elevator with apprehension. She had read in the paper that the device was safe. Obviously hundreds of people used it every day, but she had never ridden in an elevator and the thought of standing in a moving box, with a drop of five stories below her, made her nervous. She was a country mouse.

The elevator bell rang and a voice called out, "Going up." If an elevator operator could spend days going up and down in perfect safety, she thought derisively, I certainly can go up and down once. Stiffening her spine and thrusting her shoulders back, she stepped resolutely into the tiny box and watched as the operator closed first the outer door and then the inner mesh.

He moved the handle, imbedded in a brass box, to the right. Slowly the elevator rose as Esther Townsend's heart beat rapidly against her ribs and her breath came in short stabs that betrayed her fear.

"Floor please?" The uniformed operator asked impersonally, keeping his eyes forward toward the door.

"Five," Ester Townsend replied her own eyes riveted on the front of the cab as she watched the steel framework of the building pass by on the other side of the mesh door. Despite her terror, the elevator rose slowly and smoothly past one floor after another without a hitch.

"Fifth Floor," the operator announced, swinging the handle to a center position on the brass box. The cab of the elevator stopped and bounced perceptibly. Esther Townsend felt a rush of adrenalin course through her circulatory system, which caused her knees to feel weak and slightly electric. She breathed deeply and stepped quickly from the elevator.

"Thank you," she said to the elevator operator.

"Ma'm," he replied, tipping his uniform hat politely.

Mrs. Townsend moved deliberately down the corridor, reading the numbers and names painted in gold leaf on the glass windows of the doors that led into the many waiting areas on the fifth floor. Finally she found what she was looking for, opened the door and stepped in.

The office was paneled in dark brown wood. The furniture well used, institutional and also made of wood. In the late afternoon, gas lamps brightened the room even though it was still daylight.

Elihue Brown, George Soper's secretary, dressed in the standard wool suit of the office worker, stood and greeted Esther Townsend with a business like, "May I help you?"

"I am Mrs. Townsend, Mrs. George Townsend. I have an appointment with Dr. Soper," Esther Townsend explained.

"Ah, yes, Mrs. Townsend. Won't you please have a seat? Dr. Soper will be back in a few minutes," Brown replied, gesturing to a high-backed chair in the waiting area.

"Oh dear me," Mrs. Townsend replied, her voice a little fretful. "Isn't he here? I'm just a little worried about my return to the country, don't you know. It wouldn't do to be delayed. I came all the way from Oyster Bay, don't you see."

"A long trip," Brown commiserated. "They say it will be much quicker when the tunnel is finished."

"Oh my, yes. But I'm not certain about riding in a train under the water and all. Don't seem quite natural does it," she said, deciding in the moment that she should stay in a hotel over night and make the return voyage to Oyster Bay in the morning. Her eyes traveled around the office but found no distractions that could take her mind away from worrying about the long trip home. After a prolonged pause she said, "Is it true what they say in the paper?"

"Is what true, Mrs. Townsend?" Brown inquired politely.

"That the typhoid is brought on by Hudson River ice?" Mrs. Townsend replied.

Brown was about to reply when the door behind him opened and George Soper, a short, slender man with sunken cheeks and the penetrating look of a religious zealot, stepped into the room. George Soper, who sported a handsome drooping moustache, gave the impression that all his clothes had been freshly starched only that morning and that so much starch had been used that his clothes could never crinkle. From the tall stiff Arrow shirt collar, to the crease in his pants, his clothes looked as if they had just been ironed only minutes before he had walked into the room.

"Mrs. Townsend," he said, removing his gloves and offering his small narrow hand. "George Soper."

"Dr. Soper," Mrs. Townsend said, smiling graciously.

"I apologize for having kept you waiting. Won't you come in?" He held open the door to his private office for Mrs. Townsend even as he spoke to his secretary. "Would you get us some cold water, Mr. Brown?"

"Certainly Doctor," Brown replied, his tone deferential.

Soper's office was not much more interesting than his waiting room. The noticeable difference, which Mrs. Townsend could recognize even after a cursory glance, was that it was stacked from floor to ceiling with book cases that contained hundreds of leather bound, weighty tombs with titles in at least four languages.

"Chilly outside, isn't it?" Soper said, placing his homburg hat atop the coat wrack, unwrapping a scarf from his throat, removing and hanging his top coat. "May I take your coat Mrs. Townsend, you must be warm."

"Yes I am, rather," she said, smiling at him and turning her back so that he could remove her coat more easily.

There was a knock at the door.

"Come," said Soper.

Elihue Brown entered carrying a small tray on which stood two classes of ice water.

"Thank you Mr. Brown," Soper said, dismissively.

"Oyster Bay is even chillier, if I may say so, very damp on the Sound. Gets my joints something fierce, don't you know," Esther Townsend prattled as she took the chair Dr. Soper had offered before settling in behind his desk. "I was reading in the paper that your department thought the Typhoid might come from Hudson River ice. Is that true?"

"We have a great many theories about the origins of typhoid, Mrs. Townsend. River ice, like all of them, is under investigation," Soper replied solemnly. "We believe river ice carries typhoid, but we are quite convinced that it is not the cause of the infection."

"How do you investigate it?" Esther Townsend asked. She wasn't simply making small talk, although she was very skilled at the art of conversation. She was indeed genuinely interested in the subject. It was what she had come to New York and this office to talk about.

"We take samples from the cut ice when it is brought ashore before we send if off for storing. Hudson River ice is used year round throughout the city and even in parts of Long Island, and Westchester County," Soper explained.

"Indeed, we have an ice house on our property," Esther Townsend said. "That's one of the reasons I was so interested. Do you test to make certain that stored ice does not contain typhoid?"

"Indeed we do, Mrs. Townsend. You wanted to talk about a typhoid epidemic, I believe," Soper said, ending the small talk.

"They say you're the world's leading authority on typhoid, Dr. Soper," Esther Townsend said, her voice turning from polite conversation to concern.

"If one can be an authority on a miserable illness that kills thousands of people every year, strikes without warning from no established direction and for which there is no known cure, then I suppose I am an expert," said Soper bitterly. "Although I doubt that I'm the world's leading authority."

"I heard you were at Ithaca and that you turned that epidemic around," Mrs. Townsend said gravely.

"Yes," Soper replied.

"...and the same in Watertown..."

"Indeed. My secretary, Mr. Brown, informed me that you had an epidemic in Oyster Bay."

"Last summer. Only a small one. One household," Mrs. Townsend replied, fidgeting nervously with her gloves. The subject obviously upset her.

"I don't regard any incident of typhoid as small, Mrs. Townsend. Last year alone this country lost twenty-three thousand people to Typhoid Fever. When one considers that the bacillus kills only ten percent of those infected, one grasps the enormity of the problem."

Mrs. Townsend cut across his little speech, "The people in my house didn't die, Dr. Soper. They were terrible sick though. It's somethin' I never hope to see again."

"They weren't your family then?" Soper inquired.

"No, summer people who rented my house." She halted for a moment and then spoke in a rush of words that betrayed the terrible fear that had brought her to Soper's office. "I don't understand it, Dr. Soper. We don't get typhoid fever in Oyster Bay and certainly not in my house. My house is quite large, you see. I inherited it from my late husband, rest his soul. At one time I thought to sell it and invest the money. After Mr. Townsend passed, I couldn't handle the expense of running it, if the truth be known." She looked down at her gloved hands in slight embarrassment as she reached the end of her sentence

"...and the typhoid?" Soper prompted.

But Mrs. Townsend would not be distracted from the arc of her tale, "The summer that my husband passed was a bad year for real estate sales, but summer rentals have always been good in Oyster Bay. On the advice of my husband's lawyer, I leased the house to a fine young banker and his family. The rent more than met my needs for the whole year and I've been renting it every summer since. I live on the income, don't you see. The house has turned out to be a God send.

"The wealthy of New York discovered Oyster Bay some years ago, don't you see. They come out to escape the heat of the city and enjoy Long Island Sound and the company of others like themselves. Of course the popularity of the place has increased mightily since Mr. Roosevelt was elected President and established his summer White House at Sagamore Hill. The house is my income, Dr. Soper. It's important..."

"And the typhoid?" Soper prompted once again. "You had typhoid in the house?"

"This summer past, I rented the house to General Charles Henry Warren and his family. Nice people, don't you know. He's a banker. He and his wife Doris have two children. Lovely little girls, Abigail and Constance."

"The Warrens contracted typhoid?" Soper prompted again.

"They arrived with six in help. Onofrio, who takes care of the garden, comes with the place. He works year round for me. To tell you the truth I'd be lost without him."

"How many people in the household?" Soper asked, trying a different point of entry.

"Eleven in all. Fine people. Did I say the General was a Banker?"

"Yes, you told me that. Did they all contract the fever?"

"Six of the eleven were struck down including my Onofrio. It's a terrible disease, don't you know."

"Yes it is, but no one died?" Soper asked.

"Thank the Lord no, though we nearly lost Onofrio."

"Has this happened before?" Soper questioned.

"As I said, we don't get typhoid in Oyster Bay. I can't ever remember an outbreak of typhoid fever in all of the years I've live in the area, though it is situated on the

Sound so you might suppose we would get it from time to time," Mrs. Townsend replied.

"I can't say it's a story that I haven't heard a hundred times before," Soper said. "What was the cause of the outbreak?"

"That's just it," Mrs. Townsend replied. "There was no cause."

"There had to be a cause, Mrs. Townsend," Soper responded. "There's always a cause if you look closely enough. Who did the investigation?"

"The Oyster Bay Department of Health, but they didn't find anything. The authorities were ever so anxious, what with President Roosevelt and his family being in residence just across the Bay and all, but they could find nothing that caused the problem. They found traces of the disease in the septic system, which they said they expected, but no cause of the origins of the disease. That's why I'm here."

"Why you're here?" Soper asked with increased interest.

"My house was the only house in Oyster Bay to be stricken last summer or indeed any summer that I know of. I've heard about typhoid houses…"

Soper cut her off, "Typhoid houses have a long history of typhoid not just one incident in one summer, Mrs. Townsend."

"My house is my livelihood, Dr. Soper. I cannot afford to lose that income. If people think it's a typhoid house and I can't prove it's not…"

"You're afraid people will blame the house?" Soper asked, cutting her off again.

"I'm afraid word will get around that my house is a typhoid house. I'm afraid no one will rent it next season. I asked my Doctor to tell me who was the most qualified typhoid expert in New York. He named you, said that people call you 'the epidemics man,' said that if anyone could find the cause of the outbreak it would be you. So I came all this way to ask you, if you would investigate the outbreak, Dr. Soper." Mrs. Townsend sat back in her chair and waited.

"It will be extremely difficult," Soper said at last.

"I am willing to pay," Mrs. Townsend replied.

"It's not a matter of money. The epidemic occurred more than six months ago. The trail will have grown cold," Soper mused, as if contemplating whether he could overcome the difficulties of the investigation.

"Do you think you could at least give my house a clean bill of health, Doctor? A clean bill of health from a man of your reputation would really mean something to people." It was her last argument, her final chance, as she saw it, to save her house and herself.

"I could probably do that," Soper said, nodding his head in agreement.

"Thank you Dr. Soper," Mrs. Townsend said. Her wrinkled face broke into a great smile of relief. "Thank you so very much."

Chapter 4

The Investigation

It was nearing the end of February, 1907 when George Soper finally received the reports from Oyster Bay. As the dim light filtered in from the small windows in his office, he stood behind his desk; bent over, resting his hands on the deeply polished surface. He was intently studying the raft of papers spread out across the dark brown wood. The file that was the subject of intense study was titled, "Report of Typhoid Incident: George Townsend House, Oyster Bay, Long Island, New York."

His gaze slid to the bottom of the last page. The stamped words "No Apparent Cause" stood out like an accusation, or perhaps a challenge. Soper had built his reputation solving problems that had eluded others. He thought he might enjoy showing the Oyster Bay Department of Health how a real investigation should be conducted.

The diminutive Sarah Josephine Baker, M.D, just out of medical school and excited by her inclusion in the investigation, had dark brown eyes that sparkled with intelligence behind thick, rimless glasses. An attractive woman working in a man's world, she was given to hiding her youthful figure beneath warm woolen suits set off by mannish shirts and striped ties.

On this February morning she was sitting behind the desk in her small office reading a printing of the Pure Food and Drug Act. George Soper cracked open the door and stepped in. She put her finger on the line she had just read and looked up quizzically. As was her habit, she pushed her spectacles back up on her small nose, as if to better see who had been so discourteous as to enter without knocking.

When she recognized that the intruder was Soper she smiled inwardly. Soper was not a man to stand of formality when it came to junior staff.

"Grab your bag. We're taking' a trip," Soper announced, without so much as a how-do-you-do.

"And a good morning to you too," Baker smiled indulgently as she placed the papers she had been studying in a folder. "Have you read the fine print in the Pure Food and Drug Act yet?"

"I've been busy," Soper growled, as if the question had been meant as a criticism.

"Congress passed it last June," Baker persisted.

"Took them long enough," Soper groused. He wanted to be on the road, not discussing politics, which never came close to the thrill of a field investigation.

"We have some teeth at last," Baker sighed happily, standing up and moving toward the coat rack. "So where are we going at this hour of a cold and damp morning?"

"They had a typhoid epidemic in Oyster Bay, Long Island last fall with absolutely no cause," Soper replied as he looked around the office for the place she had stowed her black bag.

"Impossible," Baker responded automatically.

"I know. That's what interests me," Soper grinned.

"I don't like that word," Baker replied, donning her coat without so much as an offer of help from Soper.

"What word?" Soper asked, sounding slightly distracted.

"The word 'interests' when applied to an epidemic makes me nervous. I suppose you're going to show the local Health Department how to conduct an investigation," Baker smiled knowingly. "I thought you were managing the contaminated ice investigation?"

"Nobody needs me around to take samples. Where's your bag?" Soper responded. He sounded grumpy and impatient.

"In the cabinet," Baker replied, humor twinkling in her warm brown eyes.

"We'll need test tubes, gloves, tweezers, measuring tape, labels, pen and ink, stoppers, and whatever else I haven't thought of," Soper informed her, as he pulled out her black bag and started toward the door. "We can stop at the lab and pick up what we need on the way out."

They arrived in Oyster Bay late in the day, exhausted from the long drive over dirt roads, which had included traveling over the magnificent Brooklyn Bridge and two flat tires. Soper had insisted on driving, not only because he felt it would impress the Health Department in Oyster Bay, but because he and Josephine Baker were bringing as much scientific equipment as they could fit into the back of his car. He could, of course, have asked for the equipment from the Oyster Bay Health Department, but then it would not have been his and he didn't want to owe favors.

Soper inquired about the Townsend residence at the Grocery Store in the Moores Building. It was a relatively new structure newly made of brick following a disastrous fire in the late 1890s and stood out like a bright shiny penny. In the store they received directions along with half a dozen questions about their purpose in visiting Mrs. Townsend. They were also informed that President Roosevelt used the upstairs meeting rooms as his summer office when he was out visiting Sagamore Hill.

"A great deal more information than I needed," Soper groused.

"Really, I thought the clerk rather charming," Baker replied, laughter twinkling in her eyes once again. Soper's persistent grumpiness amused her endlessly.

Mrs. Townsend and Onofrio were waiting for them at the house. Due to the lateness of the hour and their general exhaustion from the trip, Soper decided to begin his investigation in the morning. Mrs. Townsend offered them the use of the house for the length of their stay but, out of consideration for Dr. Baker's reputation, Soper declined. They chose instead to take rooms at the Octagon Hotel which boasted central heating, a rare find even in the luxury hotels on the popular vacation spots of Long Island, self-generated electric lighting, the uniqueness of being the only octagonal hotel in all of America and a fine dining room.

They dined on roast beef, Yorkshire pudding, roast potato, pickled beets and fine wine. Baker bemoaned the fact that she couldn't live permanently with central heating and electric light. They retired early on separate floors in anticipation of a busy morning.

They got to work early after a delicious breakfast of bacon, eggs, freshly baked bread and steaming tea. Soper began his search indoors, dismantling the piping for the indoor plumbing, placing scrapings from the insides of the pipes into test tubes which he corked and labeled meticulously. He followed scraping the toilet piping with scrapings from the pipes that carried water from the attic cistern to the sinks, and from the sinks to the septic system.

Josephine Baker, dressed in her perpetual wool suit topped by a thick camel hair coat buttoned up to the neck, took samples from the privy which still was in use behind the house. She too placed her samples in test tubes, corked and labeled them carefully. Although, according to Mrs. Townsend, only Onofrio still used the privy with any regularity, because of his infection Baker expected it might be contaminated. She did not expect that the privy would contaminate the water system but she had no intention of leaving a source of possible contamination uninvestigated. They would put dye into the privy at some point and see if by watering the area the dye could be traced to the well. She next moved to the ice house which had recently been filled with new ice for the next summer but which had a residue of melt water on the ground below. If the ice had been the source of the infection the melt water should be contaminated.

To his delight Soper did not have to clamber over the sharply pitched roofs to reach the water tank. With forethought George Townsend had conveniently placed the tank in the attic when he had first installed indoor plumbing in this house. Soper lifted its lid, took samples of the contents and dropped red dye into the tank which had been designed to provide water pressure throughout the house. To his satisfaction, within the hour, water containing the red dye could be found at every sink and in every toilet in the house. He noted the fact in his case diary, a lined notebook, in which he kept notes of every epidemic. He also kept lists of each of the test tubes he and Josephine Baker had filled, corked and labeled so that he could track the results of each of them.

Outside, Onofrio had been engaged to dig up the dirt around the pipes that led from the house to the septic tank and also to expose the cesspool. Onofrio had already done this once for the Oyster Bay Department of Health Investigators so the earth was loose and easy to move. Soper had admonished him not to break the pipes as he dug, but he still checked every inch of piping carefully to make certain there was no breach.

To his satisfaction there was no trace of red dye leaking anywhere along the pipe between the house and the cesspool, but there was visible red dye in the cesspool itself. He took several samples from the cesspool, corked and labeled them.

Josephine Baker and George Soper next measured the distance from septic tank to the family well. They drew water from the well to check for dye and to test for evidence of typhoid. They would check for dye again before they left on the off chance that the well had gotten polluted as a result of any of the steps they were taking. In Ithaca, New York, a huge epidemic that had been caused by the flooding of the rivers that ran into Cayuga Lake, the infection of wells that were supposedly safe had drawn Soper's attention to the need to test all well water. Once he had made certain that the water and waste systems in the house were not the source of infection, he dropped red dye into the privy to check the possible contamination from that source.

In 1903, many rest homes that dotted the rivers that fed Cayuga Lake in upstate New York – the water source for the town of Ithaca and of Cornell University located on a hill above it. The rest homes were places where patients recovering from typhoid regularly came to regain their health. Looking for a convenient place away from their buildings, rest home owners had built their outhouses along the river banks. Even in 1903 it was well known that typhoid patients discharged bacilli in urine, but it did not occur to the owners of the rest homes that their outhouses could contaminate the rivers. Rivers were thought to clean themselves every hundred yards or so.

When the rivers had badly flooded early that winter, the water scraped the shorelines clean carrying the typhoid along with the waste down river into the city's water supply and even into the ground water that served the wells of Ithaca.

When Soper had arrived to take control of the situation, the citizens of the city of Ithaca, and the students at Cornell University, were well along in the progression of a major epidemic. To his dismay there had been a mass evacuation to other parts of the state. How many other cities were contaminated by infected people escaping the epidemic in Ithaca will never be known.

By trucking in fresh drinking water, and digging out all the deposits from upstream that now layered the city's water supply, pumping out the water supply and local septic systems and carting the refuse to a distant field, he gradually helped to end the epidemic.

The most important lesson he drew from Ithaca was that water from so-called safe wells needed to be tested.

There had been an episode in Ithaca in which a single well, which was considered to be safe, had greatly exacerbated the epidemic. Because the woman on whose property the well was located had not been properly diagnosed by her local doctor, the well had not been tested. The results had been catastrophic for more than two dozen people.

Once they had finished with the major testing, they moved on to what Soper termed his "leave no stone unturned" testing. He filled test tubes with samples from each of the now desolate flower beds, the vegetable garden and even the compost pile. Baker, for her part took scrapings from various sections of the lawn.

As they were busy with the gardens, Mrs. Townsend paid a visit to see how things were progressing. She was startled to find Soper in her garden.

"What are you looking for in the rose garden?" she asked, amusement reflected in her tone.

"Traces of contamination," Soper replied in all seriousness.

"From my front lawn?" she asked, eyeing Baker as the young Doctor knelt down to scrape the grass."

"The children might have played on the lawn and failed to properly wash their hands, Onofrio and Doris Warren handled cut flowers, the staff handled raw vegetables. I would not like to have missed the one thing that would give us the source of the infection simply because it did not seem probable," Soper responded, corking a test tube, writing a label and then logging the information in his case book with a number that corresponded to a schematic he had made of the house and grounds.

Their investigation had taken the better part of the day so they decided to leave the interviews until the next morning. Baker loaded the dozens of test tubes into the trunk of Soper's Oldsmobile and then went into the house to wash her hands. She longed to soak in a hot bath and regain feeling in her chilled toes. The bath was a reward she gave herself on her return to the Octagon.

During a dinner of roast chicken, candied yams and greenhouse salad, she and Soper discussed the day's activities in an attempt to ascertain whether they could possibly have overlooked something important. They hadn't. In complete satisfaction they went to sleep early.

The next morning they began the interviews.

"I have never treated typhoid before," Dr. Samuel Bigelow informed Soper, "Although, of course, I have read about it and studied it. We do not generally have typhoid in Oyster Bay. Indeed, no one can recall an outbreak. You must understand that there was a panic because the President was still at Sagamore Hill, but outside of Onofrio no one in town contracted the disease."

"Was there anything that suggested a source to you?"

"Nothing. The oldest daughter contracted the disease and I suppose she could have infected some of the others, but where she contracted it is a mystery," Bigelow recounted. "I was surprised at the strength of the illness. It was completely debilitating."

"That's not always the case," Soper replied. "Some people have such mild cases that they think they have simply had a slight case of diarrhea. Others die. It is unpredictable."

"I would be quite content never to see it again," Bigelow mused.

"Exactly what was the order in which the family and staff contracted the disease?" Soper asked.

"They all contracted it within a week of August 27th," Bigelow replied. "Why?"

"That would suggest that the staff did not contract it from the family, but that everyone contracted it from the same source," Soper replied thoughtfully.

"I didn't think of that," Bigelow mused.

Down the street at City Hall, Josephine Baker was busy interviewing Owen Hatfield, a gentleman with impressive mutton chops on his well-rounded cheeks, who was the entire Oyster Bay Health Department.

"I tested samples of all the pipes entering and leaving the house and could find no source that I didn't think had been contaminated by the people who had gotten sick while they resided there," he said a little defensively.

"The outhouse and the cesspool," Baker said. It was more a statement, not a question.

"Of course, and I also tested the well, the flower beds and the lawns. I have already sent copies of these files to Dr. Soper, but I made additional files for you." He handed her a thick file which she took with a smile and a thank you. "The town government is more than anxious to find the cause of the outbreak. We do not have a history of typhoid in Oyster Bay, and we do not want to develop one."

Baker nodded in full understanding. The damage that a typhoid outbreak could do to a town's economy could be devastating.

Soper and Baker left in the late morning traveling the unpaved roads from Oyster Bay back to New York City.

"The only thing that I didn't find in the report was a generalized test of clams and oysters," Soper mused. "It might have been the shell fish."

"Everyone in Oyster Bay eats clams and oysters in summer. Many of them ate them raw. No one else in the village contracted typhoid. How do we even know if the family ate clams within the incubation period? More to the point, would the help, particularly Onofrio, have eaten raw shell fish even if the family ate them? And within the family would children that age be inclined to eat them raw?" Baker argued. "Do you think anyone in the Warren family will remember if they ate clams or oysters last summer, and specifically when they ate them?"

"You'll have to ask the Charles Henry Warren family," Soper responded. "We won't know until you ask, will we."

"What are you going to do?" Baker asked, completely understanding that he was handing over the interviewing to her.

"I'm going back to testing contaminated ice. At the very least we will limit the spread of the disease if we test the ice before it is distributed to the multiple ice houses throughout the city."

"Doesn't this case interest you any more?" Baker asked, looking at him out of the corner of her eye.

"Oh, it interests me very much. We cannot stop these epidemics until we find their source. However, I expect you can cast as wide a net for this disease as I can. And I need to get back to the river ice."

It took Baker a few minutes to digest the compliment that Soper was paying her in his turning over the investigation to her. When it finally sank in she found she could barely breathe with the excitement of it.

They drove in quiet companionship. Occasionally bringing up questions they thought might be important to ask the Warren family. Baker took notes.

"Do you know the answer to why trips always seem faster on the way home?" Baker asked as the low slung buildings of the city became evident from the Brooklyn Bridge.

"No. Perhaps it's a phenomenon like the moon appearing to go backward when you drive forward."

"Maybe. A psychological rather than an optical illusion," Baker mulled.

"Interesting, I wonder if there's any science behind it," Soper contemplated.

Chapter 5

The First Clue

The Warren house was a brownstone on West 57th Street. Twenty-five feet wide and 250 feet deep, five stories high with a central stairwell that separated the front from the back of the house. Chimneys ran up the north side of the brownstone at the front and back with every room on each floor having access to the heat along an outside wall. The house was rich with deep colors of red set off by dark stained wood. Oriental rugs warmed the highly polished wooden floors. The Warrens liked the leaded glass of Tiffany Lamps and they could be found in every room. Impressionist oil paintings by Monnet and Gauguin hung beside portraits of people who Josephine Baker assumed were dead relatives. She noticed a skinny Lehmbruck in a corner, a stone head of the Laughing Buddha and stacks of leather bound books.

Her family, like the Warren's, had been collectors of fine art and books and she delighted in finding these treasures in their collection.

They were seated on velvet-covered Victorian couches in the formal living room. Baker had been busy drawing blood samples from all of the Warren family and staff. She had given them containers with which to deposit stool and urine samples and promised to return to collect them in the morning. She made sure to go over the instructions of how to label them once more so there would be no mistakes.

"It is urgently important that we know whose samples they are," she said. "It wouldn't do to have infected samples from the wrong person."

Both Warrens assured her that they would instruct the help and the children in exactly what to do. They would tell the children that this was a science project which would excite both of them greatly.

"Thank you very much for your cooperation General, Mrs. Warren," she said as she closed her medical bag in preparation for her return to the office.

"Anything to help," Warren replied. "We completely understand and sympathize with Mrs. Townsend's concerns about the house. Quite frankly we are curious about your outcomes as well. It was startling when the Department of Health in Oyster Bay could find no cause for the outbreak. Startling and a bit concerning, if you know what I mean."

"Here are the employment records you requested," Doris Warren said, offering a number of files with each staff member's name on the top.

"Thank you," Baker replied, tucking the files into her briefcase. "I'll be sure to return these after we have had them copied. Do we have blood samples from everyone on your staff that was at the Townsend house last summer? I know we have the two of you and your children and all the staff that is currently in the house." She offered Doris Warren a list of the people from whom she had drawn samples.

"Everyone except Mary and the gardener Onofrio," Doris Warren replied after studying the list carefully.

"We tested Onofrio when we were in Oyster Bay," Baker said. "Who is Mary?"

"Mary Mallon was our cook, and our savior. She was wonderful. A saint. We had seven people in the household dreadfully ill, including Doris and the children, and she cared for all of them. I had already had typhoid so I knew I wouldn't get it. I helped where I could, of course, but without Mary I don't know what I would have done."

"I think it's safe to say we couldn't have managed without her," Doris Warren agreed. "I remember the night I was bathing Constance and Mary saw that I had become ill and put me to bed immediately. She sat up night after night in the children's room sponging them and making certain that they had fresh water to drink so that I wouldn't worry and be tempted to risk my health caring for them. While in between she did the same for the staff and me."

"I remember when she came to tell us that the children were better. 'They said they were hungry,' she came into our room to inform us." Warren said, a faint smile lighting his face at the memory.

"They asked for bacon with their eggs after they'd hardly eaten for days," Doris Warren agreed, reaching for Warren's hand. "She was so happy, 'and bacon,' she said."

"They had only eaten chicken broth which Mary had spoon fed them for days," Warren said, his face turning bleak at the new memory. "She told us how chicken broth was a magic formula that would make us all better."

"Is she still with you?" Baker asked.

"Oh, no. She got us through the worst of it and then she left," Doris said sadly. "We would have kept her forever, after what she did for us, but she wouldn't hear of it. I suspect that she did not like the fact that we had an outbreak. She moved on as soon as she could."

Chapter 6
Forming the Team

George Soper's office was crowded. Soper, Josephine Baker and two Inspectors from the New York City Department of Health – Joseph Jacobs and Willard White – occupied chairs facing a blackboard that had been placed on an easel in one corner of the room. A calendar of July, August and September 1906 had been sketched on the chalkboard. Soper was standing in front of the chalkboard using a piece of white chalk as a pointer.

"Let's review," Soper said, "The Warren outbreak occurred between August 27th and September 3rd of last year." As he spoke, Soper lightly shaded in the dates of the outbreak.

"Given the known incubation period," Soper said.

"One to three weeks," Josephine Baker muttered under her breath.

Soper counted back three weeks from the 27th, "The Warrens and their staff had to have been infected before August 20th."

"But cannot have been infected much before August 6th," Jacobs added.

"Exactly!" Soper exclaimed. He drew a double line in front of August 6th.

Josephine Baker leaned forward resting her elbows on her knees, "The Warrens themselves arrived on June 15th."

Soper circled the date.

"The servants came at different times but, with one exception, they had all arrived by the 12th of June," Baker continued, consulting her notebook. "There was little coming and going. General Warren took a trip to the city on business on July 24th and 25th but no one in the household left Oyster Bay for any reason after the 25th of July."

Soper circled the dates and waited for Baker to continue.

"The only person to arrive after July 25th was a new cook, Mary Mallon. She arrived on the 4th of August to replace the original cook who had contracted appendicitis."

"Did the other servants who work for the Warrens in New York accompany them to Oyster Bay?" Jacobs asked.

"The entire staff came from New York. Only two people were hired just for the summer, the cook Mary, because of the medical emergency, and the gardener Onofrio who comes with the Townsend house. Onofrio contracted typhoid in this epidemic and nearly died," Baker reported. "The cook Mary did not."

Soper turned to the group tapping his finger on the blackboard. "What do the facts that none of the people who contracted the disease traveled out of Oyster Bay at any time between July 26th and August 27th, and there were no other known cases in the area, suggest?"

"You said that the septic tank didn't contaminate the well?" Jacobs confirmed.

"The septic tank and outhouse are infected, as one would suppose. The well was not contaminated. Pipes leading from the house toilets were contaminated as one would expect, as were the pipes leading from the sink and tub where people washed their hands and bodies. All the pipes leading from the house were intact which would make any leakage from them, which might have contaminated the well, a non-issue. The well itself was not contaminated by the outhouse which was contaminated, or by any of the lawns or gardens which were not. We did find a place behind the barn which was contaminated. Possibly Onofrio used the area as a bathroom if he was away from the house, but that too did not infect the household as it did not contaminate the well. Tests on drip water from the ice house were also negative. At this point, there was not a single means that I can see by which the infection could have been introduced to that household without infecting other people in the neighborhood. I want to know what we've missed."

"I followed up on the shell fish theory, by the way," Baker interjected.

The shell fish theory being new to the conversation, the two inspectors swung around to look at her.

"Contrary to my doubts, the family does remember the last date on which the infected members of the family and the staff ate clams. They ate raw oysters just after their arrival, out of the contamination period. Contrary to our beliefs, the staff did eat clams when the family ate them. Everyone reported loving the clam stew the cook had prepared, which means the clams had been cooked for everyone. No one had eaten oysters or clams for six weeks before the outbreak. The dish was prepared by the original cook that had come with the family, not the replacement cook. It was a specialty of hers that the family had enjoyed during other summers and which they had particularly requested. Doris Warren remembered talking about having one more clam dinner before their scheduled departure in September. Typhoid interrupted that plan. Mrs. Warren reported that they ate their clams cooked because the children didn't like eating them raw.

"Cooking them would have killed the bacillus," Jacobs remarked.

"Exactly," Baker agreed. "The only vector for infection by clams would be if they had been eaten raw, since cold does not kill the bacillus."

"That's very sad," Soper muttered almost to himself.

"What's sad?" Baker asked, picking up the comment almost like a bird dog.

"The fact that they remembered the last time they ate clams and that the clams were cooked. I rather liked that theory." Soper replied.

"Dr. Soper, you said none of the people who were infected traveled to or from Oyster Bay, what about the uninfected people?" White asked.

"I said that only Mary Mallon had traveled to the house within the incubation period," Baker replied, a tinge of irritation coloring her response.

George Soper's eyes seemed to become unfocused and his body grew very still. To those in the room it became obvious that his mind was fully engaged in examining a problem. Without explanation he moved to a table beside a bookcase where he had stacked piles of journals. Frantically he started searching through the stacks.

"I read something..." he said at last as he pulled out a journal and leafed through it. He sighed, put the journal back in the pile and picked up another.

"It wasn't in English..." he said, shifting to a different pile. He picked up and leafed through several more journals without finding what he wanted. To the members of the team, waiting to see what his apparent breakthrough would deliver, he resembled nothing more than a gopher burrowing through and discarding piles of journals.

"French? No....Italian? No .....German.... hmmmmmmm..." Soper dug deeper into a large stack near the end of the pile. He pulled out a thick, glossy covered journal with a look of triumph. He wet his finger and moved it quickly down the table of contents.

"Robert Koch... *Festschrift Zum Sechzigstan Geburstag, Neuntzien Hundert Drei,*" he read aloud. He opened to the page he wanted and scanned.

"Nobel Prize, 1905," Baker muttered to herself. Soper looked up at her and nodded.

"Koch has a theory," he said at last. "He writes that he believes it is possible that asymptomatic people..."

"No current symptoms…" Baker said. She had developed the habit of translating medical terms to the uninitiated even when the translation wasn't needed.

Soper glared at her, "…can still harbor and transmit the disease after they have recovered physically."

"We know about urinary carriers," Baker said. "However, there's nothing to suggest that anyone in the household was recovering from the disease. Recent recovery from the disease prior to moving out to Oyster Bay was one of the questions on my list."

"The evidence is not complete that someone in the household wasn't recovering," Soper replied.

"I asked whether anyone in the house had ever had typhoid," Baker said. "Charles Warren volunteered that he had once had the disease, but that had been ten years earlier. His urine tested negative. Indeed none of the household urine tested positive except for Hatti the laundress and she was one of the people infected."

"Under any circumstances Koch seems to be suggesting that an otherwise healthy person might be the source of the disease," Soper persisted.

"A carrier? That is a very frightening possibility," Willard White said. "An asymptomatic carrier could infect a whole community before we even knew he was there."

"We already know enough not to release typhoid patients from hospital until their urine tests negative," Jacobs added.

"That's very unreliable. Physicians misdiagnose typhoid all the time," White replied.

"Misdiagnosis was a major headache in the Ithaca and Watertown epidemics," Soper agreed.

"And not all doctors put patients in hospitals. Nor do they always keep them in hospital until their urine has cleared," Baker added.

"I asked each member of the staff who didn't get typhoid in this epidemic if they had ever had typhoid before and all of them replied in the negative." Baker said. "But that didn't mean they hadn't had the disease."

"I wonder if you'd get a positive Widal from an asymptomatic carrier." Jacobs pondered.

"Widal shows antigens to a bunch of diseases, how would you know it was typhoid?" White pointed out.

"How would you even begin to screen a community?" Baker wondered aloud. "What if we screened and didn't find anything?"

"If we're dealing with an asymptomatic carrier that's just what we might find," Soper replied. "Nothing."

"How about the stool?" White asked. "Could the source of infection be the stool? The septic tank and outhouse were contaminated.

"They would be contaminated by urine if typhoid was present." Baker put in.

"Stool instead of the urine?" Jacobs asked.

"Why not both?" White replied.

"Difficult to test for. Widal wouldn't work, that only looks for antigens in the blood. What would we use to test with?" Baker asked.

"Koch mentions a new culture medium in which to test fecal matter. If it works it should expand our capabilities in that direction incredibly." Soper said, holding up the journal and referring to the article.

"Send to Germany?" Jacobs asked.

"It'll take weeks... months," Baker mused.

"We've got years, Dr. Baker," Soper replied, his voice showing a firm finality. "Typhoid isn't going anywhere and neither are we."

Chapter 7
Mary Mallon

Mary Mallon strode south from the 34th Street exit near the giant new Macys Department Store and turned north into the Irish enclave of Hell's Kitchen. She walked with the long mannish gait that many who later persecuted her used as an example of her many faults.

Mary had looked in the mirror when she was a fifteen year old, newly arrived, Irish immigrant and had decided that her looks were never going to be her fortune. It would be work that would distinguish her. Not simply work, but a career of some kind on which she could build a reputation.

She had asked everyone she met in her new neighborhood about jobs that were available to the Irish. Her research had included pay, difficulty, how many people were involved in doing each job, how well each job was respected both in her community and by others. Which were the best jobs to aim for, which were most in demand?

While the Germans, who were flooding into the country at the same time, had gone primarily into shop keeping and farming, the Irish had gone into domestic service, law enforcement and labor. Not long after she had begun her research, Mary had identified cooking for the rich and powerful as the most lucrative of the domestic service positions open to women of her class and national origin. Since that time she had pursued her career with a determination and discipline that the wealthy men who paid her salary would have recognized and identified with.

She paid no attention to fashion but concentrated on expedience – dressing in simple black unless her employer dictated otherwise. She eschewed the S-shape foundation garments that were the fashion of the day because they hampered her ability to work. She wore low, thick heeled shoes that allowed her to walk quickly, striding out without being hampered by high heels. She did nothing to enhance her looks, pulling her blond hair back into a tight bun to keep it from falling into the food she worked with. The best that could be said about the way she looked and dressed was that she never posed a threat to the women who employed her and that was seen as a benefit to her career.

It was Mary's afternoon off. She stopped at her local greengrocer's to select the vegetables for the evening's dinner – picking through the apples, onions, squash, carrots and potatoes feeling for ripeness and soft spots and putting back any she didn't find satisfactory. Finally she selected onions, potatoes and carrots to use in a fine Irish stew. She picked through several flats of apples brought in from an apple cellar but decided against a dessert this time.

"Havin' a day off, Mary?" the greengrocer asked.

"More like half a day," Mary groused. Her perpetual air of grumpiness did not fool the greengrocer. If he had been asked, he would have said that it was just her way and that he found it rather funny.

"I got some good sauerkraut in yesterday," he said.

"Do I look like a damned German?" Mary replied, thickening her brogue for the retort.

"No, you look like a good cook. But the kraut goes down nice with a little pork hock no matter where ya' hale from," the grocer retorted, thickening his own Irish vowels. He could give back whatever Mary dealt out and knew she enjoyed the banter as much as he did.

"Hmph," Mary said, contemplating whether her Hal would enjoy sauerkraut with pork hock on this cold winter day or whether he would prefer his Irish stew with the familiar potatoes he liked so much. She decided on the latter. It would stick to his ribs and warm him to his toes.

She didn't bother with beer. Hal would have plenty of that on hand.

After paying for the vegetables Mary picked her way through the snowy street, moving on to the butcher shop. She purchased a pound of lamb for the stew and a rasher of bacon for Hal's breakfast.

Her next stop was the bakery where she purchased a loaf of whole wheat bread and two breakfast rolls.

Finally she stopped at the creamery where she procured a quart of milk, a half dozen eggs and a pound of butter. As a well trained cook she touched and smelled whatever she could to test for freshness, firmness and ripeness.

Loaded with string bags of groceries, Mary entered the building in which she shared an apartment with Hal Briehof. It was a dumbbell shaped tenement in which the rooms were lined up in a row, one behind the other, from street to back yard on a long thin Broadway lot just north of 36th Street. The five story houses were built in the shape of a dumbbell to allow a ventilator shaft to bring air and a bit of light to the center rooms.

The rent was cheaper on Broadway because of the noise from the traffic that rattled the building day and night, but it was a step up in tenements in that it required that every room in the back to back apartment have access to a window.

Of course the inner windows opened onto to the ventilation shaft, and the front windows opened onto the traffic, but at least, with the salary she earned, she and Hal could afford to live in it without sharing it with ten other people. The other amenity that she loved was that it had running water and indoor plumbing. Of course the water was cold and all of it needed to be heated, but it was possible to bathe in the privacy of your own kitchen instead of in the public bath houses, and it was also possible to use the privy on your own floor without sharing an outhouse with twenty other people.

Mary climbed the stairs to the fourth floor easily. She was a powerful woman in exquisite physical shape. Her heaviness was less fat than muscle and build, although most people who knew her casually thought she could lose a bit of weight. She set down the string bags filled with her purchases on the hall floor, unlocked the door to her kitchen and was immediately overwhelmed by the attentions of the German shepherd puppy she and Hal shared along with the apartment.

"About time, I'd about started thinkin' you had run off with the milkman," Hal Briehof said, greeting her with a warm hug and a long kiss that left her breathless.

"As if I'd leave you with this apartment," Mary shot back, pulling herself out of his embrace and stooping to retrieve her bundles. As she bent over to retrieve her packages Hal ran his hands over her buttocks and between her legs eliciting the response he was looking for, "Have patience ya' big lump. I have to set the stew unless ya' aren't hungry."

"Oh I'm hungry all right," Hal leered. He was often called "Red" for his russet hair and ruddy complexion, but Mary preferred to call him Hal. He was a handsome man, whose thick muscles and rough hands spoke of years of heavy physical labor. He and Mary had shared the flat for the nearly five years since they had met at a Saturday night social she had managed to attend during one of her infrequent periods of unemployment. They loved each other in spite of her steadfast refusal to let him make an honest woman of her and his insistence that it made him look bad to be, "livin' in sin."

"You just marryin' me for me money," she would retort when he asked her. In truth she made $24.00 a week to his $12.75 and it grated on him a bit, but he was grateful nonetheless.

"If I'd wanted to marry for money I'd marry a Ziegfield girl," was his constant retort. "They make $75.00 a week and they work fewer hours."

One of the reasons Mary liked taking employment out of town was because of the new luxuries of hot running water. Hers was a cold water flat which meant she not only had to lug the ice she needed to keep her butter cool up four flights of stairs, but she had to carry coal for heating and cooking as well.

Mary's apartment was near to the flush toilet in a closet-size room off the landing at the head of the stairs. She and Hal shared it with the other tenants on the same floor, a large family with several mixtures of cousins and siblings that shared the five rooms in shifts. The toilet had a water box over head that flushed when she pulled a string.

Her kitchen was large. It boasted an ice chest that stood in a space between the cabinets which rose to the ceiling with a space between the upper and lower cabinets that she used for storing jars of herbs and spices, canned fruits and other luxuries. Melted water from the ice chest had to be carried across the kitchen for storage in a large barrel which could be used for bathing and cleaning so Hal rarely bought ice unless he knew that Mary was coming home. He always considered it a good thing that he liked warm beer.

In their kitchen was a metal tub about 5 feet long which had a removable top that served as a kitchen table when the tub wasn't in use for bathing. Mary used the tub more for washing clothes than she did for washing herself. Since all the water for bathing or washing had to be heated on the coal stove, Mary and Hal only bathed once a week and used the public baths in the summer when the heat from the stove combined with the accumulated heat from the sun baked apartment served to make the kitchen temperature unbearable.

Against the other wall was an old, black, cast iron stove that stood on four legs and had six round burner tops. The tops opened with a spring-like metal handle. Coal was fed in at the left side of the stove so the hot air moved through a space under the burners heating the cast iron as it flowed to the pipe that was attached to the chimney, which served to bring the soot-filled smoke from all floors to the outside. The stove had a shelf above the burners on which Mary could place bread to rise if she was home long enough to bake.

The widest part of their apartment was twelve feet, since their railroad apartment ran down one side of the length of the building and there was another railroad apartment on the other side. The three bedrooms that formed the bar of the dumbbell were only ten feet wide because the stairs ate up five feet on each side. The center room was only eight feet in width because of the air ventilation shaft that served the three inner rooms.

Hal had turned the center bedroom into a walk-in closet, which was a luxury that was quite unnecessary since both of them had so few garments between them. With her good salary Mary could have afforded a bigger wardrobe but she was truly disinterested in clothing, a situation that suited Hal to a T. He had converted much of the closet into storage for his tools which allowed him to earn extra money from his regular day laborer job as a self-employed handyman.

Hal and Mary shared the small bedroom off the kitchen and used the other bedroom as a sewing area for Mary. They rarely used the living room at the East end of the apartment preferring to sit in the kitchen on their rare evenings together. Most everyone they knew thought their lifestyle a great waste of space, but envied them the wastage all the same.

Mary had planned to prepare their supper the minute she walked in the door but Hal had other ideas.

"If ya' don't keep your hands off me for a minute, I'll burn me stew meat," she said, slapping his hands away from her ample bosom.

"Put it on simmer. I've been lookin' forward to a little appetizer all week," Hal leered at her, reaching for her breasts again.

"Hal, me love, I want to cook ya' a real dinner while I'm here. Let me finish choppin'. Here take Lucky for a walk." She handed him a leash which he brushed aside.

"Mary, give the stew a little time to settle. Come on woman, turn down the heat. It's my turn. I've been waitin' all week."

Mary hid her smile as she set the pot on the back of the stove, "You're a royal pest, you know that?"

"Indeed I am, and ya' luv it," Hal murmured, moving behind her and kissing her neck and ear as he unfastened the buttons on her dress. "Jesus woman, you're wearin' a lot of clothes."

Mary moaned at his touch.

"I missed ya' Hal."

"At least you're in the city now. I suppose I should be grateful ya' didn't go back out to Oyster Bay. I didn't see ya' for over a month that time."

"I won't go back to Oyster Bay, Hal, not ever," Mary murmured, turning in his arms so that she could devour him with her hungry lips.

Hal prided himself on his love making. He would hold himself back from reaching a climax for hours until he had brought Mary to orgasms more than a dozen times. He often boasted that he was going for the world's record with her. And thanked his stars that he had a woman who would allow herself to enjoy what he enjoyed.

For her part, Mary thought of herself as one of the luckiest woman in the world. She had a man who made no bones about loving her, who would have been the envy of every woman she knew if they had known what a fine lover he was. She had a job that she enjoyed, that paid well and gave her great status in her community. She had the luxury of a large apartment that she could afford without sharing it with a dozen other people. She had a life that, with few exceptions, she thoroughly enjoyed. She had been able to put by money for emergencies.

She had reached a level of success which, with any luck, she believed would take both her and Hal well into old age, and she looked forward to the coming years.

Chapter 8

George Soper

George Soper's spacious ten room apartment had a view of the Hudson across the park which was down the hill from Riverside Drive. He was so consumed by his work that he rarely saw the view. Nor did he notice the elegance in which he lived.

As was his habit, and he was a man of perpetual habit, he cleaned his shoes fastidiously on the mat before the door. New York streets, with their thousands of horses, were an affront to his penchant for cleanliness. His battle lines were drawn at the front doormat. When he entered, he placed his gloves in his right hand pocket, he removed his outer clothing, starting with the woolen scarf that warmed his neck and hung them meticulously by the door.

His first stop upon entering the house was the downstairs water closet. It was a lovely room which boasted a small toilet closet that provided privacy for times when more than one person washed hands before dinner. Soper scrubbed his hands like a doctor preparing for surgery. He even employed a small brush to address whatever lurked beneath his nails. Once he had addressed all possible contamination on his hands, he dried them on a hand towel that was changed daily. Finally, he took a comb to his already neat hair.

Emerging from the water closet, he picked up his copy of the New York Times that had been laid on the front table for him and strode into his study where a roaring fire, set beside a leather wing chair, awaited his arrival. All his furniture was leather and dark wood. Those walls, which were not covered by built-in bookcases, were paneled in dark wood as well. The floors were polished and pegged wide board with oriental rugs scattered throughout. The curtains were Empire Damask bearing the distinctive Hinsdale pattern in deep red. Soper collected paintings of the places he had worked in during his many battles against typhoid. They were predominantly landscapes that included towns and villages as well as individual houses, brownstones and apartment complexes. They were constant reminders of his many successes in his battle against typhoid and his one great failure – the isolation of the cause of the disease.

On one wall of his study he had framed letters of gratitude from the important people whose lives he had so significantly impacted, as well as photographs of himself with important people affected by the outbreaks he had brought under control. There were no letters of thanks from, or photographs of, the thousands of workers, maids, and laundresses who had been saved through his efforts.

Almost as soon as he sat down, a uniformed maid, alerted by a small bell that rang in the kitchen when the front door opened, brought him a tray with goat cheese, crackers and a glass of sherry.

"We've kept your dinner, Doctor Soper. Will you be wantin' to eat in the study?" she asked, aware of his answer before she asked the question.

"Yes thank you Annie," he replied without looking up from the headlines of the evening's news. As was his habit he scanned the headlines for any news of outbreaks with an eye to how the press was treating the information provided by the New York Department of Health. He had been invited to address the American Association of Sanitary Engineers with respect to the steps he had taken to control the typhoid epidemic in Ithaca and was mentally arranging his presentation. He was making notes in a notebook when Annie brought in his dinner.

"Why don't you go up for the night Annie. I can bring the dishes into the kitchen myself," he said without looking up.

"You won't be wantin' anything else then?"

"No, I'll be fine. Thank you."

"Good night then," Annie said, backing out of the room.

Soper didn't hear her, his mind was already occupied with the proper salutation for the meeting of his peers. He barely tasted his solitary meal and only his aversion to the possibility of attracting something unwanted into his study reminded him that he had committed to carrying his own tray into the kitchen where, for the same reason, he carefully washed his dish and silverware.

He presented a stark contrast to Mary Mallon. Where Mary addressed the filth of the conditions in which she lived by ignoring them, George Soper addressed those conditions by attacking them.

Chapter 9
The War Room

In what they had come to think of as their War Room at the New York Department of Health, the team of Dr. George Soper, Dr. Sara Josephine Baker, and Inspectors Willard White and Joseph Jacobs were joined by Dr. Herman Biggs the powerful director of the New York City Department of Health. Biggs was more than curious about the progress Soper and his team were making in their pursuit of the cause of typhoid. A strong proponent of the germ theory of disease, he had already succeeded in establishing a bacteriological division within the Department of Health. Under his supervision, the division was now complete with laboratories that were already considered to have made the Department a transition institution. With Biggs' leadership and support, the young science of microbiology contributed to prove that preventing contamination from identified germs saved lives.

"Negative. Negative. Negative. Negative," Baker read off the reports of the blood, urine and stool samples she had taken from the Warren household. "If there is a carrier in this house it isn't one of the Warrens or their current staff."

"Or the well in Oyster Bay, or the cistern, or the lawn and garden fertilizer, or the house dust." Jacobs said reviewing the tests that Soper and Baker had conducted in Oyster Bay for the benefit of Dr. Biggs.

"I was really hoping for an infectious sample," Soper said.

"Have we found the cook?" Biggs asked, looking up from the written summary Soper had given him several days earlier.

"The mysterious cook? No not yet, but I think I have a lead," Soper replied.

Chapter 10
Mrs. Strikers

As George Soper walked south on Broadway, his eyes scanned the numbers and the lettering on the second floor windows of the buildings across the street. He smiled when he finally found what his was looking for. "Mrs. Strikers Employment Agency," stood out in gold lettering that could be plainly seen even from a distance. He crossed midblock and hurried to the door which gave entrance to the stairway between the millinery shop with its display of hats in all shapes and sizes and the pattern store which boasted women's high fashion straight from Paris.

A male secretary, Ernest Stevens, was filing documents in the office ante-chamber when Soper entered.

"May I help you?" he asked politely.

"Dr. George Soper of the New York Department of Health," Soper said, offering his business card.

"Mr. Daniels is expecting you, Dr. Soper," the secretary said, standing so that he could usher Soper through the door to the office protected by his desk.

James Daniels was a portly man with mutton chop whiskers and a twinkle in his green eyes.

"Would you take Dr. Soper's coat, Stephens," he said even before he had offered his hand in greeting.

Soper handed his coat and hat to the secretary and shook hands with Daniels before sitting on the opposite side of the massive desk that occupied most of the space in Daniels' office.

"I bet you didn't expect a man in this position," Daniels said with a chuckle. Laughter was an underlayment of the man's conversation.

"Are you Mrs. Strikers?" Soper asked catching onto the humor of the situation immediately.

"Indeed I am. I started as the James Daniels Agency, but no one would use me because I was a man. They assumed that I wouldn't understand their needs. After the first several months, I changed my name to Mrs. Stricker's and presto, one of the biggest domestic employment agencies in New York." Daniels' cheerful personality was infectious. "Most of the women with whom I do business think I'm my assistant and I do nothing to disabuse them of that assumption."

"And for that reason you used a married woman's name?" Soper asked, finding himself suppressing a laugh that was bubbling inside him for no apparent reason.

"Married women do not threaten other married women for starters. And, since women do the hiring in the domestic area it would be foolish of me to threaten them, Dr. Soper. They seem to trust another woman's judgment. And, the company name is a great ice breaker with men," Daniels laughed and then allowed his mouth to turn serious, "So, what brings the New York Department of Health to Mrs. Stricker's, Dr. Soper?"

"I'm conducting an investigation into an outbreak of typhoid fever in Oyster Bay, Long Island last summer. I need to talk with you about a cook named Mary Mallon," Soper replied.

"I hope there's nothing wrong with Mary, Doctor, she is one of my better cooks, and well regarded by many of New York's best families," Daniels said, his eyes growing wary.

"There's nothing selective in this investigation, Mr. Daniels. We have interviewed and tested everyone who was in the Warren household last summer with the sole exception of Mary Mallon. To date we've been unable to locate her."

Daniels pressed a buzzer on his desk and, when his secretary opened the door, he said, "Stephens, may I have

Mary Mallon's file?" His forehead creased in a frown, "I don't believe I've placed her recently. I usually keep mental track of the really good people we place."

"Well, according to Mrs. Warren you placed her in Oyster Bay last summer," Soper replied.

"For Mary, that's not recently. She likes short assignments," Daniels explained.

Stephens entered, handed Daniels the file and started to leave.

"Would you like some tea, Dr. Soper?" Daniels asked, holding up his hand as a signal for Stephens to remain.

"Cold water would be nice," Soper replied.

"Would you please bring both of us some cold water," Daniels instructed.

"Of course, Mr. Daniels," Stephens replied.

Daniels opened the file and scanned Mary's history. "I placed Mary with a family in Tuxedo in September. She left there in December when the family's regular cook returned from a trip back home to Ireland. I haven't seen her since."

Stephens returned with the water, placed the glasses on separate doilies and retreated.

"Thank you Stephens," Daniels said to the closing door.

"Is it unusual that you haven't placed her since December?" Soper asked bringing Daniels back to the subject he was there to discuss.

"No. As I said, Mary likes short assignments, prefers them in fact. Some do."

"No, I mean that she wouldn't come back to you to be placed again," Soper elucidated.

"Not unusual at all, regrettably," Daniels replied, taking a sip of his water before continuing. "Good help often work through several agencies. They also recommend each other, answer newspaper ads from the Help Wanted section and even run ads in the local papers for themselves.

I don't much like it, but it's a fact, and I won't stop placing a cook as skilled and well regarded as Mary just because she doesn't use me exclusively."

"Do you have a current address for Mary?"

"I have a Post Office Box. I believe that whomever Mary has roomed with in the past has been a bit unreliable when it comes to mail, and she works out of town a good deal. She handles everything herself."

"I'd like what you have," Soper said. Then he asked, as if as an afterthought, "Would it be possible for me to have a copy of her references?"

When Daniels looked as if he might object, Soper hastened to reassure him, "Just part of the investigation, Mr. Daniels. In scientific investigations you leave no stone unturned."

"Give me two weeks to contact the references," Daniels said, worry standing clear in his face. "I will ask for permission to release their information to you. If they object, I'm afraid you will have to go the legal route in order to obtain the information. You do understand that I need to protect my business as well as my clients."

"Of course," Soper agreed amicably. "I'll have no trouble obtaining a warrant if that will be any help."

"It would. Will this in any way impugn the reputation of my agency?" Daniels asked.

"I will make certain it doesn't," Soper assured.

"Will you let me know what you find?" Daniels inquired.

"Of course," said Soper.

"It's important if I'm recommending someone to a client, that I know as much as possible about them. Unlike the great majority of my clients, who are amazingly trusting in their hiring policies, I do investigate the people I recommend and I am extremely careful."

"I understand," Soper said, nodding his agreement. "Thank you for your help."

The two rose and shook hands. A sensation of unspoken understanding seemed to pass between them.

As Soper made his preparations to leave, he suddenly turned to Daniels as if a new idea had just occurred to him.

"One more thing," Soper said. "If Mary Mallon does contact you, would you let me know?"

"Of course," Daniels replied.

Chapter 11
The Harold Griffin Family

The brick home overlooking the Long Island Sound in Mamaroneck, New York looked as if it had stood above the water for generations. The door was answered by a liveried butler who showed Inspector Joseph Jacobs into the library. The matronly Mrs. Griffin received him reluctantly.

"I've been thinking about it since I received the call from Mrs. Strikers assistant," Mrs. Griffin said, even before he had taken the seat she had indicated. "It was a long time ago, Inspector."

"Nearly seven years, I know," Jacobs agree.

"I don't like to revisit it. 1900 was a dreadful year for this family. I lost my father from heart disease and my cousin Will almost died of typhoid. You cannot imagine how sick he was."

"Would you care to tell me about the typhoid outbreak? Typhoid is the disease we are investigating at the moment," Jacobs replied.

Chapter 12
George Soper's Office

Inspector Jacobs sat in the uncomfortable chair in front of George Soper's enormous desk as the doctor reviewed his report from the Griffin household.

"It's inconclusive," Soper said, sounding disgruntled as if the conclusions that were missing from the report were the fault of the circumstances instead of the facts themselves. "The cousin could have been infected by the outbreak in Montauk. His exposure to the outbreak at the military compound in East Hampton and his exposure to Mary Mallon are all within the incubation period. Did Mrs. Griffin slant her responses?"

"I think so," Jacobs said, "but that would be conjecture on my part."

"Did you take blood samples?" Soper asked.

"I did not need to. Mrs. Griffin acknowledged that both she and her husband had contracted typhoid in 1892 and 1895 respectively. Mary was their only household help in 1900. Once again, they told me how immensely helpful Mary had been in caring for the cousin. They liked Mary and were sorry to see her go. She left their employ as soon as the cousin was on his road to recovery."

"She certainly seems to run true to form," Soper observed, rubbing his chin. After nearly a minute he looked up and gave his orders in a rapid staccato, "Contact the Mamaroneck authorities. See what tests they ran. I don't recall any massive outbreak in the area that summer, but see if there was any infection outside of the Griffin household. At the very least, get the records of how the Mamaroneck Department of Health conducted their investigation."

Jacobs nodded respectfully, gathered his report and left Soper who was already making notes about the conversation.

Chapter 13

The Howard Wilson Family

The Howard Wilson brownstone was located on West 52nd Street. Inspector Willard White had made an appointment to interview Caroline Wilson five days earlier. Clothed in her light and frilly morning dress, Caroline served Inspector White tea in the formal living room.

"Mary left in 1902, sometime after our laundress Katharine came down with typhoid. I remember it well. Mary was incredibly helpful during the worst of Katharine's illness. Nursed her as well as attending to her cooking duties. We were eternally grateful. Then she seemed to go into a blue funk, left us within the month. So inconvenient, don't you know. She was one of the best cooks I've ever employed."

"Would it be possible for me to obtain a list of the people who were working for you in addition to Mary in 1902?" Willard asked.

"Yes, of course," Caroline Wilson replied. She rose and crossed to an elaborately carved wooden secretary, opened it, rifled through some papers and extracted an envelope which she handed to White. "I would prefer you to copy the information before you leave."

"Of course," he replied deferentially. "Are any of these servants still working for you?"

"All of them. I operate under the belief that if you change help you simply exchange problems. I seldom lose help which is why it was so strange that Mary left, particularly as she had been so helpful during the crisis with Katharine."

"I would like permission to draw blood from everyone who was in the house at the time of the outbreak including the members of the family," White said.

"Is that really necessary?" Caroline asked, indignation coloring the tone of her voice.

"It would greatly contribute to the value of our investigation," White replied keeping his own voice level and calming. "It might be the single test that solves the problem."

"Very well," she replied with a sigh that spoke volumes about the perceived inconvenience of the request.

Chapter 14
Back to Work

"How long will ya' be away this time?" Hal asked, pressing against her in an effort to entice her back into bed.

"I'm in town, I'll be home next Sunday," she smiled, ignoring his invitation.

The truth for Mary was that she missed Hal dreadfully when she was working, and missed working dreadfully when she was with Hal. She had recognized the unsettled nature of her core being early in her life and understood that Hal was the anomaly in her inclination for short assignments. She further recognized that he would only remain in her life if she left him for short periods of work and if she never married him.

"Why don't ya' stop workin' and marry me, Mary," Hall asked, as if reading her mind. He bit gently across her broad shoulders, as if to ease the tension that she held in them, and ran his hands over her large breasts, pinching her nipples until they stood erect.

She turned in his arms and looked deep into his brown eyes. "I love ya' Hal, and that's a fact. But I'm not one for the cage, ya' know. The only way to keep me is to leave the door open. You've done fine so far."

"Well then, let me give ya' something to remind ya' why ya' might want to come back," Hal said, gathering her in his arms and carrying her to the part of their bed that did not contain her suitcase. "Sweet Jesus, I do love your ass."

"Oh Hal, ya' bring such pleasure to me life," Mary managed breathlessly, before his lips covered hers, blotting out all possibility of continued talk.

Chapter 15
Mrs. Strikers Again

George Soper watched as James Daniels reviewed the list of employees that had not been tested by the Department of Health for the simple reason that they had moved from the employment of the households in which Mary Mallon had worked and had not yet been located. He was thoroughly annoyed at the transient nature of the servant class and the fact that it wasn't organized for easy access.

"We have been able to interview and test the names with check marks," Soper explained. "Are any of the others your clients?"

"Most of them have been with me at one time or another," Daniels responded after he had carefully perused the list. The names of the servants were consistently among the top in the field. It made sense. Of course, they worked for the same kinds of wealthy, well positioned people that Mary did. "As I told you, there's no loyalty to an agency when it comes to getting work."

"Do you know how we can locate them?" Soper asked, frustrated that Mary Mallon's post office box had elicited no information about her current whereabouts.

"Some of them will be easy, I know where they are presently employed off the top of my head," Daniel's replied, ringing the bell to summon Stephens. "Some will have supplied home addresses for us to contact. The others will be more difficult to locate, but not necessarily impossible. This is a different approach to placement than I usually encounter. Normally I fill places with people I know are currently available. Never before have I searched for individuals themselves."

Stephens entered the office. Daniels handed him the list, "Stephens would you pull everyone on this list who does not have a checkmark beside their name?"

"Certainly, Mr. Daniels," Stephens replied. He took the list and left the room.

"I don't know how to thank you for all your help," Soper said.

"I'm actually enjoying participating in the investigation," Daniels smiled, his jovial personality in plain view. "Tell me something, Dr. Soper. If you suspect Mary Mallon of spreading typhoid, why go to so much trouble to check everyone else?"

"When you're proving medical theories, Mr. Daniels, proving that someone isn't contagious – and therefore couldn't possibly be the source of infection – is just as important as proving that someone is and could. We don't know how this disease is transmitted yet. We don't want to close any doors until we do."

Chapter 16

The Investigation Continues

Inspector Jacobs drew a sample of blood from Elsie, the maid who had been with the Smythe family for nine years. They had retreated to one of the three small rooms at the back of the house that formed the servants' quarters of the ten room apartment in which they lived during the winter months.

"Tell me about Mary Mallon," he said, even as his eyes remained focused on the task at hand.

"I only worked with her for three ... four months," Elsie replied, her eyes betraying her discomfort at the process. "She kept to herself. I didn't know her well. She was a very good cook. We all liked her well enough. What's she done?"

"Nothing that I know of," Jacobs replied, removing the needle and releasing the constraint that had prevented blood-return from her lower arm. "I'm asking about all the people you worked with."

"Well, y've been here goin' on an hour an' the only person y've asked me about so far is Mary Mallon, so I'm thinkin' you're after her," Elsie retorted, fixing Jacobs with a knowing glance.

Chapter 17

Brownies

The kitchen at the Walter Bowen Brownstone resembled dozens of the kitchens that Mary had worked in. It had been painted white, as if white could in and of itself create cleanliness. It was the space in which cooking, as against food preparation, took place. Salads and garnishes, the creation of butter balls and celery dishes, the cutting of bread and the arrangement of rolls took place in the pantry.

The kitchen, pantry and dining room occupied the ground floor. The kitchen, with its coal-fired stove opened to the garden to provide relief from the collection of heat that the great cast iron stove created.

On this particular winter Saturday, Mary and Salina Bowen, Warren's eight year old daughter, were making the new dessert rage called 'Brownies.' Mary had found the recipe in Fannie Farmer's new *Boston Cooking-School Cook Book*. They were using the recipe as if that made the project even more special, even though in her opinion Mary thought that all she would have had to do was leave the baking powder out of any good chocolate cake recipe. As was her habit, Mary reached into the mixture with her index finger to scoop up a finger full of dough to taste it before putting it in the pans.

"It needs just a pinch of salt," she informed the wide-eyed child. "What do you think?"

Salina reached into the batter and trailed along the dent in the batter that Mary had made for her own finger full, "I think so too," she said solemnly.

Mary took a pinch of salt between her thumb and forefinger and scattered it over the batter. Salina stirred until she was certain the salt had been well distributed.

They each had another taste, this time pronouncing the batter perfect.

Mary had already greased the rectangle cake pan and dusted it with flour. Now she helped Salina pour the brownie batter into the pan, holding the bowl as the child scraped the sides.

"The rest is for you, me darlin'," Mary said, smiling, "your reward for all the help with the cookin'."

As Mary cleaned up the table, transferring the spoons and measuring cups and teaspoons to the sink and returning the flour sifter to its shelf, Salina sat on the high stool with the bowl in her lap, using her finger to transfer the last remnants of batter from the bowl to her mouth.

"I believe that y've cleaned that bowl of every morsel that remains," Mary announced, her bright blue eyes twinkling. "Here, let me clean your face and hands. You can't be goin' upstairs covered in chocolate."

Chapter 18
Expanding the Investigation

As more and more servants who had worked in the various households where Mary had once been employed were identified by an increasing number of employers, the investigation spread in ever-widening circles throughout the city.

In another luxury apartment overlooking the Hudson River Inspector White leaned forward attentively as he drew a blood sample from the lady of the house.

"Mary Mallon worked for you for only three months?"

"I would have liked to have had her stay, but she left after getting us through that awful bout with typhoid."

In another brownstone, Joseph Jacobs was taking blood samples from the butler.

"Can you tell me a little about the cook?"

"Mary? She was top of the line. Very professional. She could cook for fifty as easily as she could cook for two."

In the kitchen of a tenement Josephine Baker was taking samples from a laundress who regularly worked for the Griffin household.

"Do you remember the cook who was at the Griffin's when you got the typhoid?" she asked.

"Mary? She was a saint."

At the house in Tuxedo, New York Soper was interviewing the ruddy faced, Italian gardener who never once paused in his transfer of seedlings from flats to individual flower pots as they talked.

"Can you remember if there was ever a time that you ate a salad that Mary Mallon prepared?" Soper asked.

"Mary make-a all us help-a da food. The butler make-a da salad for da boss, Tom da foot cutta da boss' bread. But for us, Mary make."

"Would you say she was a good cook?"

"Da bes'."

Chapter 19
In The Kitchen

The family had eaten, their dishes scraped and stacked, and now it was time for the help to eat. Their conversation was lively, abuzz with the news that an immigration law had been passed which would limit the number of family members they could bring in.

"It won't affect the Irish," Mary said, setting a cut loaf of bread on the table.

"Indeed," Patrick, the butler, laughed. "Most of Ireland is already here."

Mary returned to the kitchen where she mixed the large bowl of salad greens with her hands, pouring the dressing over the greens and pushing the serving utensils into the bowl. She carried the salad to the table and, while the others busied themselves with the cold foods, returned to the kitchen to spoon large helpings of beef stew into large bowls. She set the bowls before each member of the staff before she joined them at the table.

"Has anyone seen the new cinema, 'Skating?" Patrick asked. "I hear it has a whole new technology called slow motion. We live in very exciting times."

"I would love to be in a film," Bridgette, the laundress said, her voice dreamy with longing.

"Not me," Mary said, "I'm doin' exactly what I always wanted to do."

"And doin' it well," Patrick said, tipping his spoon to her in appreciation of the excellent stew.

Chapter 20
The J. Coleman Drayton Family

J. Coleman Drayton was standing by a large brick fireplace over which hung an oil painting of a magnificent house on a bluff overlooking a tossing sea. His three piece suit made his corpulence appear more substantial than fat. He had marvelous whiskers that curled across his cheeks and was set off by his carefully rounded handlebar moustache. Josephine Baker was impressed by him. There was a power in his look, a power that broadcast his success and wealth. She felt curiously drab and small in his presence.

"This is the family house in Dark Harbor Maine," Drayton explained. His voice was startlingly deep. "Mary was with us just for that summer, sorry to say. She was a wonderful person. Couldn't have done without her. A regular angel. What a nightmare."

"Would you tell me about it?" Baker asked, her Waterman fountain pen, a gift from George Soper, poised over her notebook.

"We had a typhoid epidemic. All seven members of my household, and the nurse we hired to care for them, came down with the disease. Only Mary and I were on our feet. I tell you she was an angel. I gave her fifty dollars in addition to her salary when she left."

"Fifty dollars? That's more than a month's wage," Baker said in wonder.

"Not for Mary, she earned $24.00 a week. And I assure you she earned every penny of it."

Chapter 21
Battle Lines

In the War Room Baker and Jacobs had drawn parallel lists on the chalk board that they had installed at the end of the conference table. On one side was a list of Mary's known employers, on the second list the number of typhoid cases in each of those households.

George Soper was reading off the list as if he was reciting a dirge. "1900 Mamaroneck, New York, the cousin falls ill of typhoid. Winter 1902, New York City, the laundress contracts typhoid. Summer 1902, Dark Harbor Maine, eight cases of typhoid."

"She got a $50.00 bonus for nursing that family back to health," Baker remarked

"Sounds like paying the devil for giving his due," Jacobs joked.

"In 1903 she worked in Atlantic City, New Jersey and the family did not develop typhoid," Baker noted.

"She was the only servant in that household and both members of the family had already had the disease," White responded.

"1904 Sands Point Long Island, four cases of typhoid. Blamed it on the laundress who first contracted the disease," Soper continued.

"She's tough on laundresses," Baker noted.

"She handles raw food for the help, only cooks for the families," Soper explained. "August, 1906 the Charles Henry Warren family in Oyster Bay, three of the family, three of the help."

"If she only handled cooked food for the Warrens, and we know they didn't eat raw clams, how was it the family contracted the disease in this case?" Baker asked.

"I'm not yet certain. We'll have to revisit the Warrens," Soper replied, indicating to Baker that she should make a note to follow up on the question. "Also in 1906, Tuxedo, New York another laundress fell ill two weeks after Mary arrived."

"We're missing almost two full years," White observed.

"Are you convinced that she's a carrier, Dr. Soper?" Baker asked. She had been astonished by the findings. They had known for years that dairies, bakeries, green grocers, water systems and the like caused typhoid. They had simply identified the common source and closed it down. Never before had anyone traced the disease by following a single person and the results were startling. If they could just get the testing culture from Germany they might revolutionize the way that Health Departments handled typhoid outbreaks.

"I think she proves the theory, Dr. Baker. There are a few unanswered questions," George Soper replied contemplatively. He rubbed his fingers along his chin as he mulled over the list. "Most particularly, how was it that Constance Warren was the first to contract the disease when it should have been someone in the help?"

"And now Mary's disappeared," Baker mused.

"She shouldn't be that difficult to find. How many large, blond, blue-eyed, excellent Irish cooks can there be in New York?" Baker asked.

"Who specialize in cooking for New York's wealthiest families," Jacobs added. "The wealthy of this city are not going to like the fact that their Irish immigrant help is putting them at risk of typhoid."

"The President just banned the Japanese from immigrating," White noted.

"What has that to do with Irish immigration?" Jacobs asked.

"Just that the government is legislating immigration now," White replied defensively.

"Closing the barn door after the horse is out," Jacobs scoffed. "The country's full of Irish and they seem to like domestic service."

Soper rose from his seat at the table and walked to the window of the War Room. A panorama of lower New York spread beneath him. Office buildings, brownstones and tenements spread out as far as his eyes could see. Buildings that, at the most recent count, housed four million people and thousands upon thousands of immigrants who lived in overcrowded squalor, in filthy neighborhoods where outhouses still provided the majority of what passed for plumbing. Somewhere in all that humanity was a cook, who dispensed typhoid to the families and their servants for whom she prepared food, a cook who had disappeared into the teeming masses.

"I have a friend at the *New York Times*," Soper said, almost to himself, "I'll see if I can interest him in a story. Maybe we can flush her out with a little publicity."

"I'll check The Seeley Employment Agency. Maybe she worked for them too," Baker added. "See if we can fill in some of that two year gap."

"We can all scan the 'Situations Wanted' sections in all the papers for the past six months. Maybe she's placed an ad," White piped in.

"You won't find her if she ran an ad, only if she answered one. Let's look in the 'Help Wanted' sections, see if anyone has been looking for a cook and then contact them to see if they hired one," Jacobs replied.

"And meanwhile, our regular work goes on. We have three more new cases of Typhoid in the City that need to be investigated," Soper said, picking up a stack of paper and effectively ending the meeting.

Part II – Arrest

Chapter 22
Selina Bowen

Azaleas, in large pots that lined the steps to the front door, were in full bloom as George Soper approached the wrought iron gate which separated the Bowen brownstone from the sidewalk. He pushed the gate open, strode across the short brick courtyard, mounted the six stairs to the front door and rang the doorbell. Patrick, the butler, answered the bell, examined Soper's credentials and ushered him into the house. Soper carefully cleaned his feet on the boot scraper and the brush that were part of the entry ritual of most households and stepped into the foyer.

Ten minutes later he was seated on a plush chair opposite a heavyset, prosperous-looking man whose eyes were red and swollen with tears. A picture of Selina Bowen, the young girl who had cooked the brownies with Mary only a few weeks earlier, could be seen on the end table of the couch. There were numerous pictures of the child on the mantel of the fireplace.

"Forgive my wife's absence," Walter Bowen said quietly, his voice thick with grief. "The doctors fear my daughter may not live through the day, Dr. Soper. Our only child."

"I understand your desire to be with her Mr. Bowen, but the Department of Health must move aggressively with typhoid. You understand that we don't treat typhoid, we investigate it so that we can stop it from spreading."

"I understand," Bowen replied.

"I only have a few questions, I'll try to be brief," Soper said. "Now, who else beside the maid Bridgett, who was sent to Roosevelt Hospital, you, your wife and daughter are presently in your household?"

"My butler Patrick, who let you in. Selina's nanny Colleen, the upstairs and downstairs maids Edna and Bertha who live in the servant's quarters," Bowen listed. "My driver Frank and the footman George who live off premises but come every day as does my laundress Ruby, and the cook, Mary who also lives in-house."

Soper looked up suddenly like a pointer scenting game. Bowen didn't notice.

"The cook Mary, has she been with you long?"

"No, a few weeks only," Bowen replied. "She's very good with my daughter. She's nursed her night and day. We couldn't have done without her."

"Does this Mary have a last name?" Soper asked.

"Mallow, Mandon, Mellon, something like that. My wife would know," Bowen responded, his distraction still showing plain in his eyes.

"May I meet her?" Soper asked.

"Of course," Bowen replied. "She's in the kitchen."

Chapter 23

Mary and Soper

Mary Mallon was standing at the kitchen table chopping fresh parsley when Bowen and Soper pushed through the swinging door.

"Ahhhh. Here she is. Mary, there's someone here who wants to see you," Bowen said, by dint of an introduction.

"See me?" she said. The idea that her employer would accompany anyone who wanted to see her made Mary's knees turn to jelly.

"Yes," Bowen replied.

"Come to the front door?" Mary asked, fear visible in her bright blue eyes.

"He came on another matter," Bowen assured her, finally understanding the situation from her point of view. "It's all right Mary."

"Mary Mallon," Soper breathed, his thrill at standing in the presence of the object of so many months of effort was palpable.

"I don't know you sir," Mary said warily. The temptation to turn and run was almost irresistible.

"You are Mary Mallon?" Soper said.

"I don't know this man, Mr. Bowen," Mary replied, pleading for explanation with her frightened eyes.

"It's all right Mary," Bowen reassured her. "He's a Doctor."

Mary and Soper stood facing each other with Mary's fear and discomfort standing like a wall between them.

"Well, why don't I leave the two of you to your little conversation and I will go back to my daughter,"

Bowen said at last, figuring that removing himself from the room might lift some of Mary's fear.

"Thank you," Soper responded, never once taking his eyes from Mary. It was as if he believed that she might disappear if he released her from his stare.

"Who are you, mister?" Mary said at last.

"Dr. George Soper, New York Department of Health," Soper responded.

"Department of Health?" Mary said, the level of concern rising like a tide, "To see me? Why? I'm healthy. I got me certificate from the immigration people to prove it."

"Yes. I'm sure you do," Soper replied. "Do you think I could have a word with you?"

Mary felt like snapping at him, what the hell did he think they were having, but she bit back the remark and said instead, "I'm very busy, sir."

"This won't take long," Soper replied.

"I'm workin'," she said, a frown creasing her forehead.

"It's very important," Soper insisted.

Mary felt her temper rising, "So's me work. I don't have time for idle conversation. There's a child that's dreadful sick in this house."

"I assure you this conversation is not idle," Soper insisted.

"Oh, all right," Mary capitulated. "But be quick. I wouldn't want the family disturbed. There's a terrible illness here you know."

"Yes, I know," Soper said.

"Have a chair then," Mary offered.

"Thank you," Soper replied pulling one of the straight back chairs from the servants' dining table over to the kitchen table where Mary was preparing stew.

"Would you like to wet your whistle then?" Mary asked, assuming the role of hostess in her kitchen.

"No....no, thank you," Soper said. The idea of drinking anything that had been touched by Mary Mallon was abhorrent to his core being. "I'm fine."

"It's no trouble," Mary insisted. "The tea's steeped. There are scones on the tray. I baked 'em fresh this mornin'."

"No. No, thank you," Soper said, searching franticly for an excuse to avoid her offer. "I don't eat sweets much."

"Some cold water then?" said Mary with a sigh of annoyance.

"Thank you anyway, Miss Mallon," Soper replied

"Mrs. Mallon," Mary said.

"Mrs. Mallon?" Soper replied, puzzlement standing plain in his face.

"I'm a widow," Mary explained.

"I'm sorry," Soper said.

"Ahhh, it happened a long while back," Mary said, shrugging her broad shoulders as if the whole subject was of no matter. She pulled a colander filled with pealed potatoes toward her and started to cut them into half-inch squares.

"Mrs. Mallon," Soper blurted at last. "I need to talk to you about your typhoid."

"Me typhoid?" Mary asked, looking up from her work, puzzlement standing clear on her plain face. "I don't have typhoid, I never have."

"No," Soper said. "The maid Bridgette and little Miss Bowen do though."

"Ahhh yes," Mary said sadly, attacking the potatoes with renewed vigor. "The little one's in a very bad way. It always takes the children so hard. Terrible disease the typhoid. I hate it."

"And you've seen a lot of it," Soper said quietly.

"And what might you be meanin' by that?" Mary asked, her voice taking on an aggressive edge. She dumped the potato squares into a large cast iron stewing pot.

"I've been searching for you for a long time, Mary Mallon," Soper said, his voice lethally quiet.

Mary's hands halted midway toward the carrots that were laid out on the cutting board, "For me?"

"Yes." Soper replied. "You see I've met General Warren and his family, the Griffins, Coleman Drayton, Henry Gilsey, the Wilsons and the Johnsons. Members of my staff and I have spoken with nearly every family you've worked for since 1900."

"Why?" Mary whispered, her body frozen with fear.

"Well, it's a little hard to explain," Soper said, chuckling a bit as if to ease the tension.

"Try Doctor," Mary said, the terror standing stark in her voice.

"It's possible, just possible you understand," Soper said, "that you are the source of all this typhoid."

"What are you sayin'?" Mary gasped.

"There's a theory advanced by Dr. Robert Koch, the man who won the Nobel Prize for medicine last year. The theory states that people, perhaps people like yourself, people who had typhoid without the usual symptoms, and may not even have been aware that they ever had the disease, may still be able to transmit the disease to others," Soper explained.

"I don't understand," Mary said.

"It's still a theory," Soper began.

"What do you mean by a theory?" Mary asked, the frustration rising in her voice.

"Something we strongly believe, but we still have to prove to be true," Soper replied.

"A wild guess ya' mean," Mary shot back.

"An educated guess," Soper corrected.

"Are you sayin' that you *guess* I give typhoid to people?" Mary asked, anger replacing the fear. "Is that what you're sayin'? Here in this house with a child lyin' upstairs close to death. And you tellin' me, who's lost more from this disease than you can possibly imagine, that you *guess* I'm the cause of it?

"Well, not exactly," Soper stammered, wondering how he had lost control of this conversation so completely.

"Then exactly what are you sayin', Dr. Soper?" Mary said her face pinched with rage.

"Based on years of medical observation, we have developed the theory..." Soper began.

"The theory. Ahhhh, yes, the theory..." Mary cut in, disdain clear in her tone.

"There may be typhoid bacilli in your Gastrointestinal tract," Soper explained, reverting to the language of science in his defense against her rage.

"Ba-what?" Mary said, the fury of frustration growing with each moment.

"Bacilli. Little rod-shaped germs that cause typhoid. They're very small. You can't see them with the naked eye," Soper explained pedantically.

"In me where?" Mary demanded.

"In your gall bladder," Soper replied.

"That's not what you said the first time," Mary fairly snarled at him.

"Well, the gall bladder releases bilirubin into your small intestines as part of the digestive process. You do know about the small intestine?" Soper said.

"Don't you be talkin' down to me, Dr. Soper, just because you're a medical man and all," Mary snapped. "I'm not stupid, you know."

"I'm not a medical man," Soper said.

"You're a Doctor from the Department of Health but you're not a medical man?" Mary exclaimed. "Then what are ya', pray tell?"

"I'm a Doctor of Sanitary Engineering," Soper explained.

"And what exactly does that mean?" Mary replied, the power of her anger filling the room.

"I study... I study sewage systems," Soper could just imagine how this was going to be interpreted by the irate woman who had gone back to chopping carrots with an energy that was almost threatening.

"Pipes?" Mary asked, a look of utter confusion flitting across her angry face.

"Septic Systems and the diseases that are involved with them," Soper corrected.

"Now let me get this all clear," Mary said her brogue thickening perceptibly as she punctuated each sentence by violently sticking cloves into a peeled onion. "You're a Doctor from the Department of Health but you're not a medical man. You study pipes and drains. And you're here, as an expert in pipes and drains, to tell me that you *guess* I'm givin' little babies typhoid because I've got some invisible rods in me belly. Is that what you're tellin' me, *Mister* Soper?"

"*Doctor* Soper," Soper corrected. "Not exactly. The rods are germs, germs cause the disease. You know about germs?"

"Dirty water and bad milk give a person typhoid, Mister Soper. Everybody knows that," Mary retorted placing the onion in the stewing pot with the potatoes and carrots.

"Let me explain. It's the germs in the dirty water and bad milk that give a person typhoid," Soper elucidated, trying to keep his voice calm and without a trace of condescension. "Water and milk by themselves don't transmit the disease."

"And what does all that have to do with me?" Mary asked, reaching for a cloth bag into which she started to push parsley, bay leaf and whole pepper corns.

"Well, the germs have to come from somewhere. In this case we think they come from you," Soper explained. "You see, every time you use the toilet..."

"The what?" Mary interjected, outrage standing clear in her voice. She was so incensed that she actually threw the bag of herbs into the pot.

"The toilet... the bathroom... the privy..." Soper replied in exasperation.

"We don't mention these places in polite company," Mary scolded. "You're talkin' dirty to me in me own kitchen. Shame on you, *Mister* Soper."

"It's *Doctor* Soper, Mrs. Mallon. Toilets and septic systems are part of my investigation. I didn't mean to embarrass you," Soper said trying desperately to regain control of the situation.

"Oh, is this where the drainage pipes come in?" Mary asked, sarcasm standing straight in her voice. She pulled the piece of chuck steak toward her and aggressively began to carve it into inch-thick squares.

"Well, yes," Soper said, seeing an opportunity to return to the science of what he was trying to explain. "You see, there is a chance that some of the bacilli..."

"The wa...?" Mary exclaimed in exasperation.

"The germs," he corrected. "Yes. Well, there is a chance that they get on your hands when you use the toi-toilet."

She opened her mouth as if to object and he hurried on, "You haven't done anything wrong. You can't see them."

He watched Mary relax a little and pressed his advantage.

"Then, when you handle food, you transmit, ...uh, pass these germs to the people you cook for and make them sick," he saw that what he was explaining had dawned on her and watched as a deep red suffused the skin of her pale face. "Oh you don't mean to..."

Without even being aware of the fact that she had a butcher knife in one hand and a carving fork in the other, she waved her hands as if to cut him into little pieces, "You're tellin' me that I'm a dirty person who kills children with germs ya can't see that're inside me belly? Is that what you're tellin' me? You, who calls himself a doctor from the Department of Health. The expert in pipes and drains?"

"Well...no...not exactly... but... yes. Any time you handle raw food – vegetables, or fruits, or even parsley for the meat – anything that isn't cooked, there's a chance that you might be spreading this disease." Soper said, talking as fast as he could.

In a stumbling fury Mary thrust the carving fork toward him, "Get out."

Soper jumped up from the kitchen chair and backed away from her, "Mrs. Mallon..."

Mary advanced, threatening him with the carving fork, "How dare you come here accusin' me of spreadin' that dreadful illness?"

"Mrs. Mallon you don't have to worry. I'll make it right for you. I'll write a book about you. I'll make you famous," Soper blurted.

Mary advanced, waving the fork at him, "Famous!" she fairly screamed her derision.

"I won't use your name if you don't want me to. You can have all the money from the book to live on. Just come in for some tests." Soper pleaded.

"Out!" Mary shouted.

"Just a few tests – blood, urine, stool. To find out if what Koch has written is true. To find out if you are indeed a typhoid carrier." Soper knew he was making things worse but he couldn't stop himself.

"Doctors. Tests. Self-important bunch the lot of ya', pretendin' to know what you don't know. But you don't save the little ones, do ya'? You just let 'em die in their own filth, their little bodies burnin' up with fever," Mary's fury was so great she could barely breathe. "I have no use for you or your tests and your book. Now get out!"

"All right, all right," Soper said, hurrying toward the back door. "But there are some things, some simple precautions that you should take in order to protect other people. You'll have to stop cooking of course..."

"OUT!!!" Mary roared.

"At least don't handle any raw foods," Soper said, backing across the stoop to the back stairs.

"Out!" Mary growled.

"You'd be stopping the typhoid that has followed you for so many years," he said, the fear in his voice infuriating him.

"Out!" Mary repeated, gesturing with the carving fork again.

"Think of the people you'd be saving. Mrs. Mallon, Mary, please," he pleaded as he backed down the stairs toward the sidewalk.

"Out!" Mary said, forcing him toward the gate.

"Mrs. Mallon..." Soper tried once more, his hand on the gate.

"Don't come back, *Mister* Soper," Mary said between clenched teeth. "Don't come back."

"At least scrub your hands before handling food," he managed.

The gate clanged shut behind him.

Mary turned her back to him, her body rigid with rage. She strode toward the house without a backward glance.

Back in the kitchen she leaned against the door, eyes closed, consciously slowing her breathing. When she had calmed a bit, she opened her eyes, pushed herself away from the door and returned to the kitchen table. She set down the carving fork and butcher knife and reached for the container in which she kept the flour. On automatic, as her thoughts raged through her mind, she scooped out a handful of flour with her hand. Suddenly she went white with shock as she realized what she was doing. She stopped, looked in horror at her hand and walked quickly to the kitchen sink.

At the sink she dumped the flour, picked up a bar of soap and a small brush and scrubbed her hands again and again. When she was sure they were absolutely clean, she dried them with a clean towel before returning to the kitchen table. Once there, she reached into the container, scooped the handful of flour and scattered it on the cutting board. Next she sprinkled salt and pepper into the flour, and began dipping the meat into the mixture, coating it on all sides.

When the squares of beef were coated with flour, she placed a large cast iron frying pan on the stove and scooped some lard from a container that she kept nearby for frying. After the lard had begun crackling, she tossed the stew meat into the frying pan and quickly seared it on all sides. As she cooked, she thought about all the things she would like to have said to George Soper. It was always that way. The good things that she should have said were sure to come to her late, well after the time she should have said them.

She removed the frying pan from the fire, and tossed the sizzling meat into the stew pot with the vegetables. She added a vegetable stock that she had prepared earlier in the day to cover the mixings and set the pot on the front of the stove, allowing the stock to heat quickly.

As the stew heated, Mary washed her hands again, scrubbing them violently. Next, she placed a bowl on a tray and spooned in some vegetable broth from another pot that had been simmering for several hours. She put two cups, a teapot, a sugar bowl, a small cream pitcher and the plate of scones on the tray as well.

The stew was steaming nicely now, and she moved it to the back of the stove where it was cooler so that it would simmer slowly without cooking away the liquid. Then she lifted the tray and carried it to the stairway that allowed the servants access to the second floor.

Upstairs Mary entered Selina's bedroom carrying the tray. She put her load down on the child's bureau and poured a cup of tea.

"Here ya' are Mrs. Bowen," Mary said, spooning two teaspoons of sugar into the cup of tea and handing it to the exhausted woman. "Have a cup'a tea. I'll spell ya' with the child. I made her some broth. Maybe we can keep it in her long enough to do some good. She put one teaspoon of sugar and a little cream in the other cup and handed it to Mr. Bowen who was standing by the window.

"Thank you Mary," he said. "Did your talk with Dr. Soper go well?

"Just fine, Mr. Bowen, thank you," Mary replied.

"God bless you, Mary," Mrs. Bowen murmured, sipping her tea. "We couldn't have done without you."

While the Bowens drank their tea and nibbled half heartedly on the scones, Mary picked up a clean wash cloth, dipped it into a washing bowl that sat on a table by the window, poured cool water into it and applied the wet cloth to the Selina's fevered forehead.

The Bowens finished their snack and Mrs. Bowen sighed with exhaustion.

"Why don't ya' lie down for a bit," Mary suggested. "I'll sit with Selina for awhile."

"Thank you, Mary." Mr. Bowen said, helping his exhausted wife rise from the chair in which she had been sitting for hours. He put his arm around her and led her from the room.

Mary sat down in the chair that Mrs. Bowen had just vacated, pulled it closer to the bed and began to spoon the warm broth into the child's mouth.

"There y'are darlin' this'll make ya' better," she crooned. "It has to make ya' better."

Chapter 24
Mary Found

Dr. Josephine Baker was still wearing her lab coat as she sat behind her desk reading the latest typhoid report from New Rochelle. They were making progress on tracking the outbreak, having narrowed the search to a dairy on the Boston Post Road. Her mind kept straying to Mary Mallon and what testing the elusive cook might do to the search for the cause of typhoid.

George Soper, coat tails flapping, his hat askew, virtually exploded into her office, "I found her."

"Who?" Baker asked, although in her heart of hearts she already knew the answer.

"Mary Mallon. The cook," Soper said his eyes alight with excitement.

"That's wonderful. Where?" Baker asked. Soper's excitement infected her so that she found she had to stand as well.

"At the Walter Bowen's," Soper replied. "I went there to begin preliminary tests on their typhoid outbreak and there she was, big as life. Just standing there in the kitchen. She claims she never had typhoid, by the way."

"Do you think that's possible?" Baker asked.

"No, I don't think so. I suspect she doesn't know she had it. For all we know she might have contracted it in her mother's womb. But if we are ever able to test her, and find the way this disease is transmitted, we may very well have changed the world of medicine," Soper paused for breath. "She chased me out of the house with a carving fork."

"No," Baker breathed, feeling her eyes widen in astonishment.

"Yes," Soper insisted.

"What did you tell her, Dr. Soper?" Baker asked, wondering what Soper could possibly have said that would have caused Mary Mallon to attack a representative of the Department of Health. Immigrants were generally quite careful in their dealings with authority.

"Nothing special," Soper replied.

"But you did talk to her?" Baker persisted.

"Yes," Soper said, growing defensive.

"Well, what did you tell her?" Baker asked.

"Only that we wanted her to come in for some tests," Soper mumbled.

"And she attacked you with a carving fork?" Baker said, doubt standing plain on her face.

"I don't think..." Soper said. He paused and then started in a new direction. "I thought she would so happy to learn that there might be a way to stop the typhoid that's plagued her so..."

"So you told her she was a carrier?" Baker asked.

"Well... yes, sort of. I told her we had a theory," Soper replied

"A theory," Baker said, her eyebrows traveling an inch up her forehead. "What else did you tell her?"

"That there were ways to protect against the spread of the disease..." Soper said hedging his responses.

"...and?"

"That I wanted to write a book about her, but I didn't have to use her name and she could have all the money from the book to live on..." Soper said, rushing his explanation.

"...and?" Baker pressed.

"And that of course she would have to give up cooking," Soper said at last.

"And that's when she came at you with the carving fork?" Baker said, her eyes twinkling with barely suppressed laughter.

"I suppose I could have been a bit more diplomatic," Soper said.

"What did you say about the tests?" Baker asked.

"Perhaps she would be more receptive if you spoke to her woman-to-woman,' Soper suggested, "I've never been much good talking to women, you know."

"You've always been good with me," Baker replied, relenting on the interrogation.

"I don't think of you as a..." Soper stopped himself as the implications of what he was saying sunk in.

"You're absolutely right," Baker laughed. "You're not much good at talking to women."

Chapter 25
The Chemist

Mary sat in a leather chair in the chemist's shop. The man who supplied the medicines for her neighborhood had drawn blood from her arm seven days earlier and now he had results.
"We sent your blood sample to the Ferguson Laboratory. It is the most renowned in the city."
"What were the results?" Mary asked. She was impatient for the news.
"The Widal is a difficult test to interpret," the gray haired man informed her, looking at her over the reading glasses that sat perched on the end of his long nose. "It detects exposure to a number of diseases but for typhoid I would expect a four fold increase in the titer or a conversion from one reaction to another in the same titer. I did not find this reaction in your blood sample."
"Which means?" Mary asked, trying not to show the annoyance that she felt at these men of education who would never talk plain English to her.
"Which means that I cannot detect any sign that you have ever been infected with the typhoid bacillus," the chemist said.
Mary heaved a sigh of relief. She felt the tension drain out of her broad shoulders.
"Would ya' be willin' to put that findin' in writin'?" she asked.
"Of course," he replied. He went to his roll top desk and searched for a pad that carried the title of his chemist's shop with the sign of the mortar and pestle at the top. He wrote his findings on the pad and signed with a flourish at the bottom. "That will be "$1.00, Mrs. Mallon."

"Best dollar I ever spent," she said, her horsy face splitting into a wide grin. Once again she thanked her stars that she was so well paid that she could afford to pay a whole dollar for a signature on a piece of paper.

Chapter 26
Baker and Mary

A Hansom Cab delivered Sarah Josephine Baker to the front door of the brick tenement on Broadway near 36th Street. Behind her the heavy traffic with its commercial drays, private carriages and increasing numbers of automobiles, rattled the windows of the building. The neighborhood was filled with small shops that carried everything a community would need; green grocers, bakers, butcher shops, clothiers, milliners and more.

Baker was a small, trim woman who on this day was dressed conservatively in herringbone tweed. Tweed had fallen out of fashion but she liked it when the weather was cold. Josephine Baker was confident enough in herself to wear what she liked even in the face of fashion. A striped tie sat under her throat between the high starched collars of her white Arrow shirt. She wore high button shoes, kidskin gloves and a small square hat that pulled down on her forehead. Sunlight glinted off her rimless glasses. In her right hand she carried the black bag that identified her as a medical doctor. She was not sure why she had brought it. However, given the argument Mary had had with Soper, she thought it might come in handy.

Baker opened the outside door to the building, stepped inside of the tiny foyer that kept the wind out of the hall and read the names on the mail boxes. When she came to the box marked "Superintendent" she pushed a button. The Superintendent came down stairs. Her clothes were stained from work, her hair was disheveled. She leaned insolently against the jam blocking Baker's entrance.

"May I help ya'?" she asked in a voice that did not invite a positive answer.

"Is Mary Mallon living here?" Baker asked.

"And what would the likes of you be wantin' with our Mary?" the Super asked, folding her arms across her chest and examining Baker insolently from heat-to-toe.

"I'm Dr. S. Josephine Baker, an Inspector for the New York Department of Health," Baker replied, holding out her Department of Health credentials in their black wallet.

"What's she done?" the Super interrupted in a slightly more pleasant tone. She did not like the idea of a visit from the Department of Health, and was worrying about whether her initial attitude would cause trouble.

"Nothing," Baker said calmly. She was well accustomed to people challenging her. It came with being a woman in a man's world. "I need to speak to her is all."

The Super pursed her lips considering how much trouble she would bring on herself if she didn't rat out Mary, "She's on the third floor in the back, right side."

"Thank you," Baker responded, moving around the Super to gain entrance to the building's interior. Slowly she made her way upstairs, losing her breath as she climbed and thinking to herself that she really ought to take the stairs more often. When she reached the fourth floor, which the super had called the third floor, she knocked at the door on the right side.

"Who is it?" a woman's voice demanded.

"Dr. S. Josephine Baker, New York Department of Health," Baker replied deliberately adding a level of authority to her words. "Is Mary Mallon at home?"

"Do I know ya'?" the woman's voice replied. The door stayed closed.

"No. No you don't," Baker said, leaning forward as if shortening the distance between them would make a difference. "May I speak with you please, Mrs. Mallon?"

"Who are ya' again?" Mary asked, delaying the inevitable.

"I'm a medical doctor with the New York Department of Health," Baker responded. "I have my credentials here if you would like to see them."

"Not another one," Mary sighed. "Are you a specialist in drainage pipes as well?"

"I'm a medical doctor, Mrs. Mallon. Please, it's very important that I speak to you."

"Go away," Mary snapped.

"Mrs. Mallon, it is really important that we talk," Baker pleaded.

Mary opened the door a crack. Baker could just see one bright blue eye. "I've done nothing' wrong," she said.

"I know that," Baker replied. "And I want to make certain it stays that way."

The door crashed open, revealing an irate woman with her hands on her hips and her blond head cocked to the right, "And just what would ya' be meanin' by that?"

Baker took a step back totally intimidated by Mary's great size. "I mean that if you spread a disease you don't know you're spreading you're innocent. If you spread a disease in the full knowledge that you're spreading it... well, that could be a crime."

"What do you want with me?" Mary asked taking a deep breath as she worked to control her temper.

Baker now noticed Hal and Lucky. Hal was holding Lucky by his scruff. The hair on the huge dog's back was standing up as he made himself larger in order to defend his family. Baker felt her hands start to shake and hoped that she wasn't showing how intimidated she actually was.

"I simply want to ask you to let me run some tests," she explained. "Did Dr. Soper explain to you about Robert Koch's theories on typhoid carriers?"

"*Mister* Soper, the pipe and drain specialist, told me he *guessed* I was givin' the world typhoid because I was a dirty person with rods in me belly," Mary hissed. Baker could cheerfully have strangled Soper in that moment. How could the man have botched the interview to the extent reflected in this conversation? No wonder this woman was resisting testing.

Mary picked up a copy of The *New York Times*.

"Now the little shite puts me name in the paper and goes behind me back to me agencies to be sure they won't be usin' me again," Mary's righteous anger blazed, suffusing her face with rage. "By the time you're through persecutin' me Miss Baker, I'll be lucky if I can get a job cleanin' out them toilets your so damned fond of."

"Mary..." Baker stammered.

"Mrs. Mallon to you," Mary said with dignity.

"Mrs. Mallon," Baker corrected. "I know how this all must seem to you, but it's really not the way it looks."

"Well now, how is it then if it's not the way it looks?" Mary asked and for the first time Baker became aware of her natural intelligence as well as her massive size. "Is Mister Soper a medical man?"

"Well, not in the strict sense, but..." Baker said faltering in the face of Mary's rectitude.

"Did he put this Editorial in the Paper?" Mary demanded.

"Well, yes, but..." Baker spluttered.

"Has the doctor who is not a doctor been talking about me to me agencies and me former employers?" Mary insisted.

"Well, yes... but not exclusively," Baker implored.

"And what in heaven's name is that supposed to mean?" Mary said, her voice becoming strident.

"It means that we're asking everyone who has come in contact with the Warren and Bowen families to take some simple tests," Baker explained, back again on firm ground.

"Everyone?" Mary asked, disbelief standing stark on her face.

"Well, not exactly everyone, but..." Baker heard it all come out wrong.

"Get out of me house, *Miss* Baker." Mary growled.

"We're not testing anyone who knows they have already had typhoid," Baker hurried to explain. "They would already prove positive to the tests. Other than those people we are testing everyone."

"Get out before I throw ya' out." Mary said, lowering her head like a bull about to charge.

"Please..." Baker said.

Mary picked up a metal rod. Lucky, taking his cue from Mary, began to growl.

"Out," Mary said, lifting the rod like a cudgel.

"Oh, oh my..." Baker whimpered, taking a step backward.

"Out!" Mary yelled.

Baker backed up until her heel hit the banister. She turned, cast a last look at the threatening woman at the door, and scurried down the stairs.

"For your information, Miss Baker," Mary called after her. "I had meself tested by a reputable chemist with a test called a Widal. He found nothin' and I have the paper with his signature to prove it."

Chapter 27

A Hal Moment

Mary slammed the door and turned to Hal, hands on hips, arms akimbo.

"Aren't ya' afraid of me; the dreaded typhoid carrier?" she demanded bitterly.

Hal gave her his most rakish smile and cocked his left eyebrow, "Come here."

He wrapped her in his arms and pulled her down onto the couch making a meal of her ear, "I like a bit of danger. Adds to the excitement."

"Oh Hal. How could I live without ya'?" Mary moaned, growing breathless as he reached under her skirt running his work-coarsened hands up the inside of her thigh. "How is it ya' stay with me when I'm away so often?'

"I live in hope. Besides which I could hardly be expected to perform the way ya' like it if ya' were here all the time. I have to rest between visits."

She threw her head back with laughter. "Ya' are a right rogue," she said, the sparkle in her eye turning her almost attractive.

"Come on now woman, I don't have all that many hours that I can waste any of 'em on conversation," he said, pulling at the buttons of her shirt.

She relaxed under him, letting him slowly undress her as was their ritual.

Chapter 28

Arrest

It was early morning. Outside the Bowen brownstone, a paper boy could be heard crying the headlines at the corner. A milkman was delivering milk, the clank of the bottles in his carrying case audible above the din of the city.

A horse-drawn ambulance pulled up in front of the tall narrow house. Dr. S. Josephine Baker stepped out of the front of the ambulance and looked up toward the building. She picked up her black bag and crossed to the wrought iron gate that separated the house from the sidewalk. Three burly police officers and two ambulance attendants followed her at a short distance.

"You've got the warrant?" Baker asked the Sergeant, betraying her nervousness.

"Yes Ma'am," the Sergeant who led the group muttered softly.

"Remember, she's not a criminal," Baker instructed. "She's being taken to the Willard Park Hospital for Contagious Diseases for tests. She's done nothing wrong."

"Yes, Ma'am," the Sergeant replied, his tone slightly defensive.

They moved toward the door in a phalanx. Why did they need three officers in addition to the regular ambulance drivers if the subject of the warrant was just a patient being taken to a hospital, he asked himself. Someone wasn't telling him what he needed to know and he resented the lack of communication. It put him and his men in danger. Anything that put them in danger he found offensive.

Inside the house in the pantry where Patrick, the butler was polishing silver, the doorbell could be heard signaling someone was calling at the front door. Unexpected visitors were not the norm at this time of mourning, and he wondered who on earth could be calling, particularly at this hour of the morning.

Patrick sighed, removed his apron, and cleaned his hands on a towel that he kept on the table for that purpose. He hurried toward the front door as the bell rang again.

"I'm coming," he muttered. "Hold your horses."

"May I help you," His greeting died on his tongue at the sight of the petite woman flanked by three large police officers.

"Good morning," Josephine Baker said, flashing her Department of Health identification, "I'm Dr. S. Josephine Baker of the New York Department of Health. Is Mary Mallon here?"

Behind Patrick, Edna the downstairs maid had been dusting. Without a word she turned and moved quickly and silently through the swinging door into the pantry. She crossed the pantry at a run and burst into the kitchen.

"Mary, the police are here for ya'," Edna stammered, fear thickening her tongue. "Run."

Mary didn't say a word. With her face set in a grim mask, she turned and walked quickly to the back door. She lifted her coat from its hook beside the door, pushed her thick arms into the sleeves, pulled it up and around her broad shoulders and buttoned it. As she walked she pulled her wool scarf around her neck. Assured that she would be warm in the chill winter air, she quickened her pace as she hurried out onto the short patio that led to the frozen grass and patches of snow that formed the back yard.

The seven people in the pantry with whom she worked watched her go. Without a word they went back to their tasks as if nothing had happened to disrupt their morning routine.

At the front door, Patrick was pushed aside by the three burly police officers, who rapidly disappeared into the back hall toward the kitchen.

"Wait," Patrick exclaimed. "You can't just enter the house like this."

"Excuse me, uh – sir," Josephine Baker blurted, alarmed at the turn the event was taking. "I'm terribly sorry for the intrusion. We do however have a warrant for Mary Mallon's arrest."

"Arrest?" the butler exclaimed, "Our Mary? What's she done?"

"Nothing," Baker replied, "Nothing at all. We need to test her, that's all. She has refused to cooperate. Please. Here is the warrant. I'm an investigator for the New York Department of Health."

"We've had a death in this house," Patrick exclaimed. "We do not need police officers trampin' through, disturbin' the family."

"Yes I know," Baker replied. "That's why we need to talk to Mary. I promise we will take care to be quiet."

She pushed past Patrick and caught up with the officers and attendants as they moved into the kitchen. "Under no circumstances may you disturb the family," she said harshly to the Police.

The Sergeant gave her a quick look that spoke volumes. These officers knew how to behave in the homes of New York's rich and powerful. They knew who could be bullied and who must be left undisturbed.

The three officers entered the kitchen. They were amazed at the quiet in the pantry, where all the help were busy with their duties, apparently completely unaware of the drama playing out in their midst.

"Is Mary Mallon here?" the Sergeant asked, his investigatory energy out of step with the atmosphere in the room.

None of the help responded. They kept their eyes on the task in front of them and their hands busy.

"Is she?" the Sergeant insisted.

"No sir," George the footman responded at last. He was the next in the pecking order after Patrick who had gone to alert Walter Bowen.

The officers pushed past him, rushing into the kitchen, opening then slamming closet and cupboard doors. Finding no trace of Mary beyond the kitchen table where a leg of lamb sat ready to be studded with slivers of garlic and rubbed with rosemary and lemon. Finally they found the door that opened to the back and rushed through it.

Mary Mallon raced through the garden. She could imagine the pandemonium behind her and knew that time was not on her side.

The back yard was large enough to use for dinner parties in the summer. It was set off by a high fence at the back that was too high to jump. There was a gate in the back that could be used for access, but it was locked and she did not have a key. She was completely trapped.

Under an oak tree that spread its branches from the corner of the garden was a picnic table surrounded by six chairs. She pulled a chair from its place in the bank of shallow snow that had not melted since the last winter storm, placed it against the fence and, taking a running jump, reached forward, grabbed at the top of the fence, and with great effort pulled herself up and over.

The policemen and ambulance attendants exited the back door, crossed the patio and begin searching the yard.

"She came this way. Here's her footprints," The youngest of the officers called out as he approached the oak tree.

"She can't have got out," the officer with red hair and freckles announced. "Look at that fence."

"Search the yard," the officer in charge shouted. "I want no stone unturned."

In the alley on the other side of the fence, Mary tried every door that opened into the narrow space between the buildings, muffling the rattling sounds as much as possible. Under the stairs framing the back of another brownstone that faced 54th Street she finally found a line of cabinets that served as a storage area for the house. She rattled two doors that were locked before she found one that was empty and open. Quickly she forced her large body into the narrow, icy, dark space that smelled of mold and animal droppings. In her haste to turn and shut the door, she failed to notice the small edge of the hem of her long, wide skirt that had caught on the corner of the door and ripped. It was the only evidence of her passing.

The Sergeant stared at the spot in the ground where the chair had once been held in the frozen grip of the snow. "By God, she's a wonder. Look, she must have pulled the chair out of here by herself."
"And got over the fence," the youngest officer mused. "I don't know many men who could hoist themselves over a fence that high – and she's wearing skirts and petticoats."
Josephine Baker hurried up to where the officers were staring at Mary's route of escape, "Well, don't just stand there marveling, find her. She can't get far. She's left her purse."
"Spread out," the Sergeant ordered. "She's wearin' light blue calico. She can't stay out long, it's freezin'."
"Unless, of course, she took a coat," Baker observed.
"Yes," the Sergeant responded, "unless she did that."
In the pantry George reported back to Patrick. "She's disappeared."

"What do ya' think she did?" Edna whispered.

"That Doctor said she had done nothing wrong, they wanted her for some tests is all," Patrick said.

"Well, I wouldn't want to see Mary arrested if she's done nothin' wrong." George replied.

Josephine Baker leaned against the ambulance blowing warmth on her frozen hands. It had been five hours since Mary had vanished over the fence in the back of the Bowen brownstone. The search was lasting far longer than she had dreamed possible and she was impressed with the tenacity of the police.

Assuming that Mary had gone to ground in the time she had had to escape, the officers had made a grid of the alleys that fed off the back of the house and had poked into every nook and cranny they could find. They had knocked on doors and asked the members of the staffs of the other brownstones if they had seen a large, blond woman in blue calico uniform with an apron. She might have been wearing a coat. No one had seen her. They had tested that doors and windows were locked, even searched inside rubbish bins and boxes.

Periodically the Sergeant would report to Baker. She could tell the tolling of the hours by the number of reports.

"Any luck?" she would ask.

"None so far," was the constant reply.

"It's been five hours," Baker observed. "Where could she be hiding?"

"Ten miles away if you ask me," the officer replied. "Maybe we should go to her digs."

"Maybe later," Baker responded. "Keep searching another half hour. If we don't find her here, I don't believe we'll ever catch her."

Inside the alley where a number of boxes had been stacked against a row of storage cabinets under a stairway, the youngest police office suddenly stopped and looked.

Caught on the corner of one of the wooden doors was a small piece of light blue and white. The little square of cloth was barely discernible, but it looked like it just might be part of the hem of a skirt.

"Hey Red," the young officer called to his red headed partner, gesturing with his arm to come and look at something. He held his finger to his lips in a sign that Red should be quiet.

"What is it?" Red whispered.

Again, the young officer gestured for silence and Red dropped his voice to a lower whisper.

"You see somethin'?"

The young officer pointed at the bit of blue hooked at the base of the door just visible behind the stacks of boxes.

"We'll have to move these boxes. You do that while I fetch the Sergeant." Red whispered.

The young officer lifted a box as quietly as possible and stacked it on top of several other boxes two cabinets down the line. By the time Red had returned with the Sergeant he had all the boxes in front of the cabinet with the suspicious blue cloth hooked on the door, and the cabinets on each side of it, cleared of boxes.

"You go right. I'll go left. You open the door," Red whispered.

The young officer nodded. The two officers separated and took up their positions on either side of the cabinet while the sergeant placed himself several feet in front of it. The young officer grasped the door handle and pulled. The door opened and Mary jumped out fists flailing.

"Bastards!" she screamed, rage built of fear giving her a strength that even she didn't know she possessed. She raked her nails, like talons, at Red's ruddy face. He was so shocked by the attack that she completely bowled him over and nearly succeeded in making good her escape.

The young police officer grabbed her around the waist, holding on for dear life. Red finally managed to imprison her hands, while the Sergeant tackled her around the knees trying in vane to bring her down to the ground.

"Here she is," the young officer yelled to the ambulance personnel and Baker. "Help. Help."

Mary kicked and flailed, landing a blow on the shoulder of the Sergeant that almost immobilized him.

Red, with a streak of bloody nail marks down his face, tightened his grasp on her arms. He reached out with his right foot, caught her behind her legs, pushing and tripping her backward. Off balance, the two officers were able to wrestle her to the ground.

Even lying on her back on the cobblestones, Mary was vicious. She landed several well placed punches and kicks before the Sergeant landed on her legs.

From the distance came the sound of running feet and shouting.

"Don't hurt her." Baker screamed.

"Don't hurt her!!? The Sergeant shouted back.

"Fookin' bastards!" Mary grunted.

One of the ambulance drivers joined the wrestling match as the other raced back to his vehicle to grab a stretcher and restraining straps. The four men holding Mary down were having a very difficult time controlling the large, strong and fiercely struggling woman. They managed to keep her on the ground, but they couldn't seem to keep her from doing an immense amount of damage to each of them and it looked like she might escape at any minute. She punched, kicked and bit. The men shouted and grunted as she landed blow after blow against their exposed limbs.

"Hold her down there," Red yelled.

"She bit me!" the young officer yelled.

"Don't let go of..... Mary, Mother of God" said the Sergeant as Mary freed her right foot and caught him in the knee cap with the sharp toe of her leather boot.

"I'm bleedin'," the young officer complained.

"I don't care what you're doin', grab her....uuuuhhh, the Sergeant screamed in pain as Mary nailed him in the groin.

The second ambulance driver ran up with the stretcher and Baker yelled at him, "Get the ambulance and bring it around. We'll never get her all the way over there."

She could see that even though the wrestling match appeared to be very uneven, the four men could not keep Mary under control. They wrestled her onto the stretcher, but they couldn't keep her there long enough to free a hand to get the straps on her. Finally in desperation, Baker ran over to the struggling mass and simply sat down on Mary's stomach, robbing the woman of air.

"Mary dear," Baker pleaded. "Stop it now. We only want to run some tests. It's nothing bad. For goodness sake, we don't want to hurt you."

Mary glared at Baker, her face contorted by such rage that Baker flinched.

It was not apparent to Mary that no one wanted to hurt her. She heaved her body in a renewed effort to escape, but was now restrained with a man on each limb and Baker sitting on her stomach. Her breath came in short, wild gasps. She resembled nothing less than a trapped wild animal.

Chapter 29

Second Meeting

Willard Park Hospital for Infectious Disease looked every inch a prison. Its small windows were barred, the doors locked and the rooms were cramped and institutional. The only privacy afforded to the occupants was a toilet with a door.

Although she was completely healthy; Mary was kept in an isolation room with a small window in the door for observation.

George Soper stood back as an attendant, dressed in white, unlocked the door.

Inside the room with its cot, chair and table, Mary – dressed in a long, white, terry cloth robe – stood by the window staring out across the East River.

"Good morning Mary," Soper said.

Mary looked up, identified him and turned back to the view across the river.

"No one means you harm, Mary. I've come to talk with you and see if between us we can't get you out of here," Soper said, making his voice as pleasant as he knew how. "The specimens, and yes I know about your objections, but the specimens prove that you have caused dozens of cases of typhoid. Because of you, countless people have suffered and at least one little girl is dead."

Mary hunched her shoulders as if defending herself against attack. Her face grew pinched with anger.

"No one thinks you did this on purpose, but it's happened just the same. I'll tell you how you do it if you like." When Mary didn't respond he continued, "When you go to the toilet, the germs that grow inside your body get on your fingers. You can't see them, but they're there none-the-less. When you handle food, the germs are transferred to anything that you handle that is not cooked: salad, fruit, bread, even parsley and other garnishes. People who eat the food swallow the germs and get sick. You don't keep your hands clean enough, Mary. You can never keep them clean enough to be handling food for other people.

"On the good side, we believe that if you pursue some housekeeping trade other than cooking, you could lead a relatively normal life."

Mary snorted through her nose feeling the anger build in her even while realizing that getting angry would make things worse.

"Actually, I have some really good news in all of this," Soper said, trying to sound patient. "We have developed a new theory. Well yes, an educated guess, but we've developed the theory that the germs are probably growing in your gall bladder. I believe I mentioned this when we first met at the Bowen's brownstone."

Mary flicked a hate-filled glance at him. She turned back to the window.

"The best way to get rid of the germs is simply to get rid of the gall bladder. People don't need their gall bladders to keep them alive any more than they need their appendix. There are many people living perfectly normal lives without them. All you have to do is have your gall bladder removed and you can be free."

The offer sounded good to Soper, but when he saw the set of Mary's shoulders he knew that he had lost. Perhaps she realized how risky abdominal surgery was. Perhaps she had heard about the death rate they were experiencing even with required surgery. She wasn't dumb, he knew that, but she didn't know much about science. What she knew and what she guessed was a mystery.

"Now, I don't know how long the Department of Health intends to keep you here," Soper persisted. "I suppose that depends on you. But I can help you gain release. I would like to help. If you will just answer my few questions, have your little operation, the authorities and I will do everything we can to reinstate you back into society. You can answer my questions can't you?"

Mary didn't reply and he interpreted her silence as permission to continue.

"When did you have typhoid? You did have typhoid, no matter what you say," Soper said.

Mary remained silent, her arms folded across her chest, her jaw clenched.

"At least tell me how many outbreaks and cases you've seen?"

Mary turned abruptly from the window and drew her robe tight around her body. Soper shrank back against the door anticipating physical attack. Mary glared at him. Then, without taking her eyes from his face, she walked in dignified silence to the bathroom. She entered the tiny room, closed the door behind her and locked it.

Chapter 30
JAMA

Josephine Baker was reading a copy of the June 15, 1907 *Journal of the American Medical Association.* Visible at the top of the page was the title, "The Work of a Chronic Typhoid Germ Distributor" by George A. Soper, Ph.D.

"You're famous, Dr. Soper," Baker said, smiling up at him, "The man who rid the world of Typhoid Mary."

"I prefer to think of myself as the man who discovered the a-symptomatic typhoid carrier," Soper admonished.

"Congratulations on this article. It will make a tremendous difference in the control of this disease, no matter what you're called," Baker laughed. "Did you see that we've found another carrier?"

"Fred Moersch – confectioner. He has actually infected and killed more people than Mary Mallon," Soper replied.

"The Department of Health found him a job as a plumber's assistant," Baker informed him.

"Well, he has a sick wife and five children, we can't let him abandon his family by keeping him in a hospital," Soper replied. "And again, he was fully cooperative."

"And Mary?" Baker asked.

"She may claim to be Mrs. Mallon, but we can find no trace of a family, only a boyfriend with whom she lives out of wedlock," Soper said, his face growing pinched with disapproval.

Baker refrained from stating what she was thinking. She had worked too hard, and struggled against too much bias in her own life to come to the defense of Mary Mallon even though she was quite certain that Mary would not now be traveling to a hospital in the middle of the East River had she been a man with a family.

Chapter 31
North Brother Island

The Tugboat Gladys K. pulled up to the dock on North Brother Island. Mary, her wrists in handcuffs, stood defiantly by the gangplank between three burly police officers as the boat docked.

The gangplank was pushed out onto the dock and Mary strode ashore in rebellious dignity. Her face was under such rigid control that it looked as if it had been carved in stone. Her escort hurried to catch up to her.

In the distance, beached on the rocky shore, her eyes found the burned out hull of the General Slocum, a once-white, three-decked, side-wheeler with twin stacks that had carried tourists around New York Island before it had caught fire in 1904.

"See that hull over there?" the tallest of her escorts growled at her. "That there's the General Slocum. Its captain noticed a small fire on one of the decks way back up the river there at 125th Street. Instead of dockin', he steamed full ahead lookin' for a safe place to beach. He steamed all the way up here to North Brother Island, streamin' burn victims in his path. 1,034 people died that day. Have you killed that many people, Mary Mallon?"

Mary didn't respond immediately. Only when she had her feet planted firmly on the ground did she turn to glare at her tormentor, her face a mask of disdain.

"Not yet I haven't," she stated.

Chapter 32

Soper's Interim

George Soper's face looked up from the cover of *The Journal of Sanitary Engineers*. His articles on the discovery of Typhoid Mary had by this time appeared in dozens of journals and newspapers. His reputation as a typhoid expert had been greatly expanded to the reputation of *the* typhoid expert, though of course typhoid epidemics were a thing of the past now. Josephine Baker had been correct in her prediction. He had become world famous as the man who discovered Typhoid Mary.

His reputation had translated into public appearances and speaking engagements. He had already been the keynote speaker at numerous conventions as a result of his success in Ithaca and Watertown, most importantly at the American Association of Sanitary Engineers. With the advent of discovering Typhoid Mary his lecture schedule was full and his bank balance had swollen.

"Mr. Chairman, distinguished colleagues, my fellow sanitarians," he intoned, looking at the faces of his peers. He was an excellent speaker, and the audience sat in rapt attention as he described his investigation of the house in Oyster Bay and his elimination of those who could have infected the family during the incubation period.

It was clear that he enjoyed his fame. As he spoke he controlled the history of Mary Mallon and colored it with his version of who she was.

Chapter 33
Mary's Interim

    Riverside Hospital on North Brother Island, like its sister hospital on Roosevelt Island, resembled a multi storied factory with a tall smoke stack that served the laundry. There were few buildings on the island outside the hospital itself and the dormitories for the staff. One notable exception, near the end of the island, was an isolated cottage close to the water's edge. The cottage was small and white. In summer, blankets of climbing roses on white trellises decorated the entrance on each side of the door. Bright orange geraniums in pots dotted the short path to the house. It was a pleasant place with its back turned toward the towering structure behind it giving it a view of the distant city on the other side of the river.
    Inside the cottage Mary sat in a large comfortable chair which had been placed beside a window for better light. She was reading a novel. Her dog Lucky who had been brought to her by Hal during his only visit to see her, was sitting beside her. She absently stroked his ears.
    The knock on the door surprised her. As sweet and pleasant as her cottage was, she was kept in total isolation from outside visitors, patients in the hospital and hospital staff. Only the presence of Lucky kept her from going mad.
    "Who is it?" Mary called.
    "And who would ya' be thinkin' it was," Aggie joked. The red headed Aggie, a rebel by nature, was Mary's only visitor during the endless days of isolation to which she had been subjected; the only one brave enough, or curious enough, to sneak over to see her.
    "Come in then," Mary said, her strong horsy face breaking into a grin of welcome.

Aggie popped her head around the door. She was dish faced with curly red hair, weak blue eyes, freckles, a kind smile and bad teeth. Mary was so much larger than she was it sometimes seemed as if Aggie might be Mary's little girl instead of a woman of almost equal age.

"Oh, I do so like this cottage, Mary. Such a special treat it is separated from the rest of the hospital and all. Almost feels like havin' your own little house without all the expenses and such."

"More like a leper colony," Mary groused. "Except that they only have one leper in it. Imagine, with all the thousands of people with typhoid in the city and they've only isolated one of them as contagious. I suppose I should feel honored for all the attention, but I'd really rather prefer to be workin'."

"At least they've given ya' livin' quarters the rest of us would die for," Aggie said. She was a merry person who could find a silver lining in every situation. Mary was glad of her company.

"They built it for the superintendent of nurses ya' know," Mary said, a wry smile pulling at the edges of her wide mouth.

"Can you imagine how put out she must have been when they give it to you?" Aggie's happy laugh filled the cottage.

"She can have it back any time she wants it," Mary replied, her own humor asserting itself.

"How ya' do go on," Aggie said, after the laughter had worn itself out. "I brought some tea. We can sit and chat for a bit if ya' like."

She opened a basket she had brought with her, placed two cups on Mary's table and poured the tea. "I put sugar in it while it was steepin'."

"Jesus, girl. You'd never make it as a cook in the big houses pollutin' tea with sugar during the steepin' process," Mary chided. She knew why Aggie had brought her own tea. Nothing that Mary Mallon touched with her germ infested hands could be allowed near the lips of another human being.

"They say me tuberculosis is about cleared up," Aggie said, turning to the reason she had risked making a visit to Mary. "I'll be leavin' soon. What about you Mary?"

"They're keepin' on at me to let them cut me up as the price of gettin' out," Mary said bitterly.

"Whatever for?" Aggie asked, her eyes widening with disbelief.

"They say they think that the typhoid might just be livin' in me gall bladder. They have a theory ... you know what a theory is Aggie? A theory is a wild guess that men with education use against women without it. I'm here in this place because of a theory," Mary growled, the flush of anger coloring her horsey face.

"No..." Aggie breathed.

"That was a different theory, of course," Mary said. "They have a lot of theories these men. Now they have the theory that I'll be cured of spreadin' the typhoid that I don't have if I let them cut away parts of me body. Of course they think I don't know how many people they've killed with their little operations. Men of education have little regard for the likes of us, Aggie."

"Are ya' goin' to let them?" Aggie asked.

Mary gave her a look that spoke volumes.

"They'll keep you here, y' know," Aggie said, her voice grave. "They'll keep ya' here and throw away the key."

"I'll fight them," Mary said.

"How?" Aggie asked.

"I don't know. I'll find a way," Mary said, her face grim. "I've been writin' letters you know."

"I'll help ya' if I can," Aggie said.

"Ahhhh, thank ya' Aggie, you're a good friend. I'll miss ya' and that's a fact," Mary said, her smile sad. The empty feeling in her stomach betrayed a well of hopelessness that weighed her down.

Chapter 34

George Francis O'Neill

Mary was hot and sweaty when she returned to her cottage from her brisk morning walk around the circumference of North Brother Island. She unwound her hair from its protective scarf, moved to the kitchen sink, pumped several inches of water into it, and began to wash her hair. When she had soaped her hair completely, she used the pump again, dipped her head under the cold running water and rinsed the suds into the basin. When she had finished rinsing her hair, she wrapped her wet tresses in a terrycloth turban. The hot pink of her face had cooled with the washing of her hair. Next she set about to wash her face, hands and under arms.

As she was finishing her wash, she heard a knock at the door.

"Who is it?" Mary called, pulling her bodice back into place and buttoning her blouse.

"George Francis O'Neill, Mrs. Mallon," a man's voice replied. "May I come in?"

"What would ya' be wantin' with me, George Francis O'Neill?" Mary asked in a challenging voice. She opened the door to reveal a man she had never met before. Outside of Aggie, and the occasional doctor or nurse, she had not had a single visitor since the first days of the onset of her isolation on the island when Hal had brought Lucky. The presence of a complete stranger was, to say the least, unexpected.

"She told me you were feisty," O'Neill said, a wide grin lighting his face as if she had told a funny story.

"Who told ya' I was feisty?" Mary demanded.

"Aggie," O'Neill replied, watching Mary closely to assess her response to the name.

"Aggie, who worked in the laundry?" Mary asked in complete surprise.

"The same," O'Neill replied. "She came to work in my house some weeks ago. When she learned what I do for a living she told me your story."

"And just why did she seem to think my story would be of interest to you?" Mary asked, placing her clenched fists on her hips, elbows defiantly akimbo. "And how did ya' manage to get permission to visit me when no one else in the world is allowed to violate me isolation?"

"How would you like to get out of here?" O'Neill asked, his eyes sparkling at the ridiculousness of his question.

Mary just stared at him.

"I'm a lawyer, Mrs. Mallon," O'Neill announced. "I specialize in medical injustice. From what I've heard from Aggie, you've had just about all the injustice one woman should have to endure."

"I can't afford ya', Mr. O'Neill," Mary said, bitterness reflected in her face and body.

"My fees are covered by the Hearst newspaper, Mrs. Mallon."

"The newspaper?" Mary asked. "I wrote them a letter but they never responded."

"What has been done to you is a scandal, Mrs. Mallon. Mr. Hearst feels that yours is a wrong that should be righted," O'Neill explained.

Chapter 35

Day In Court

On June 9, 1909, Mary and George O'Neill walked up the fifty white steps to the entrance of Manhattan's Tweed Courthouse where the Supreme Court of New York was in session. The steps led to a landing covered by a triangle portico supported by four massive Corinthian columns. Just behind the columns three enormous arched wooden doors gave entrance to the bright white, three and one-half story building. If the building itself had not been intimidating, the octagonal rotunda, that stretched three stories to the roof where a skylight flooded the great hall with brilliant daylight, took Mary's breath away.

She had worn her best dress, a black, light wool, tailor-made skirt that did not quite touch the ground, a high collared white shirt, held stiff with whale bone, a red man's tie and a fitted jacket that matched the skirt. For once she had piled her blond hair into something that resembled the fashion of the day instead of pulling it back into its normal utilitarian bun. She felt uncomfortable as she walked through the crowd of mostly men. They looked important, with preoccupied faces. Most people looked neither to the left nor the right as they hurried up the cast iron stairs on the east and west sides of the rotunda to the courtrooms where they conducted their business.

Mary's hearing was scheduled to be heard in room 202, a grand room of gold and white with a wooden balcony surrounding the courtroom like a second story. Once again the theme of arches and columns was carried out in classic style. In all her life, despite her many years of cooking for the wealthy of New York, she had never imagined seeing anything as magnificent and intimidating.

Dr. Baker, Dr. Jacobs, Dr. White and Dr. William Park sat close together on the left side of the aisle behind George Soper and Penrod Smith, the lawyer for the Department of Health, who were seated at the left hand table. O'Neill and Mary sat at the table on the right facing the judge. Behind Mary, Aggie and Hal were seated close enough to provide support. The courtroom was packed with curious spectators who had come to hear and be part of the case of the notorious Typhoid Mary.

The Bailiff rose from his table at the foot of the bench and cried, "All rise. Hear ye. Hear ye. All those having business before this session of the New York Supreme Court step forward and you shall be heard."

Supreme Court Justice, Mitchell Erlanger entered from his quarters behind the bench, looking every inch the successful man he was with his portly bearing, his black robe and his substantial gray whiskers. He sat and gaveled the court to order.

"This is a habeas corpus proceeding?" he asked O'Neill.

"Yes, your Honor," O'Neill replied, rising to address the judge.

"I've read your preliminary documents, Gentlemen. Why don't you proceed, Mr. Smith"

"Thank you, your Honor," Penrod Smith replied, rising to address the court. "The case of Mary Mallon is very special. While it is true that Mary Mallon has not been convicted of any crime, the New York City Department of Health feels justified in removing her from the general population under the imminent-peril section of the New York City Charter and the health laws of the State of New York to whit, Section 1169 which says, 'The board of health shall use all reasonable means for ascertaining the existence and cause of disease or peril to life or health, and for averting the same, throughout the city.' And Section 1170 which states, 'Said board may remove or cause to be removed to a proper place to be by it designated, any person sick with any contagious, pestilential or infectious disease; shall have exclusive charge and control of the hospitals for the treatment of such cases.'

"Your Honor, what we are talking about is the right of the New York City Department of Health to place a woman who has been known to infect more than a dozen men, women and children with typhoid. At least one child has died as a result of her contact with the defendant," Penrod Smith said, finishing his opening statement and sitting down. He knew that there were some giant holes in this case concerning whether existing law could be applied to healthy carriers of disease, since they were not specifically covered by statute. He was careful to limit his argument to the habeas corpus aspects of the case, hoping that O'Neill would not question the Department of Health's jurisdiction.

"Thank you Mr. Smith. Mr. O'Neill, are you prepared to address the Court?"

O'Neill rose, "Yes, Your Honor. Mary Mallon, who you see before you, is a professional cook – was a professional cook – living and working in New York City. She is a healthy woman in her prime, with more than a dozen tests carried out by the renowned Ferguson Laboratory which have all proven negative for typhoid. Mrs. Mallon paid for these tests herself out of her concerns about the accusations by the Department of Health.

"She has been incarcerated in solitary confinement at the Riverside Hospital on North Brother Island, with only the company of her dog, because she is the only such healthy typhoid carrier quarantined on the island although statistically there should be several hundred such carriers in New York." O'Neill went on to describe Mary's arrest and incarceration in detail before beginning the summary of his argument. "At no time was Mary Mallon allowed representation by counsel. At no time was she granted as much as a hearing. At no time was she found guilty of a crime. She hasn't even been accused of a crime.

Nevertheless, she has been arrested, tried, convicted and incarcerated in solitary confinement for over two years without sentence, term limit or reprieve.

"The Fifth Amendment to the United States Constitution, among other things, clearly states that no person shall be deprived of life, liberty or property without due process of law; due process, Your Honor, not Divine Right. What this hearing is really about, Your Honor, is the important question – do we or do we not have a Constitution of the United States of America? And if we do, is the New York Department of Health exempt from living within its framework?" O'Neill sat down. His opening remarks had been powerful, he knew that. His question was whether they would hold up against the medical evidence that the Department of Health would present.

"Thank you Mr. O'Neill. Mr. Smith are you prepared to present your case to the Court?" Erlanger inquired.

"Yes, Your Honor," Smith replied.

The interrogations began with Dr. Robert A. Park, who had conducted more than one hundred tests on Mary Mallon during her incarceration.

"Mary Mallon can best be described as a human culture tube," Park reported.

"Culture Tube?" Mr. Smith prompted.

"A glass container in which we grow the germs that cause disease in our laboratories," Park replied.

"Mary Mallon grows germs?" Smith emphasized using the question to underline the statement.

"Objection," O'Neill shouted. "Conjecture."

"Sustained," the Judge replied.

"Would you please explain what you mean, Dr. Park," Smith said.

"Yes," Park replied. "Every day her body manufactures germs so plentiful and so dangerous that she could infect whole cities under the proper circumstances. For all we know she might have done that already."

"Objection," O'Neill interjected. "Speculation."

"Sustained," the Judge replied. "Strike that last sentence. Please confine your comments to the facts, Dr. Park."

The interrogation continued describing in detail the tests that the Department of Health had conducted on Mary Mallon's stool and urine samples.

When it came time for O'Neill to cross examine Dr. Park he had only two questions. The first was had Mary Mallon ever given permission for her stool and urine samples to be tested. To which the answer was, "No." And had Dr. Park ever tested Mallon samples that had been negative for typhoid, to which the answer was, "Yes."

"In fact, Dr. Park, you tested Mary 163 times and only 120 of those tests were positive which means that nearly one third of the tests were negative?"

"73% were positive," Park replied.

"But if nearly one third of the tests were negative, and all of the Ferguson Laboratory tests were negative, does that not call into question the veracity of the testing?"

"Not in the slightest," Park replied. "There could be a hundred reasons for the negative results."

"You just don't happen to know what they are," O'Neill replied.

"Objection!" Penrod Smith exclaimed.

"Sustained," the Judge responded.

As time passed, George Soper was called to the stand. Once again Smith took him away from the limited question of whether Mary had been improperly arrested and into the question of how he had discovered that she was a typhoid carrier.

"Beside the fact that typhoid outbreaks occurred in six of the seven households that we have been able to identify as places in which Mary Mallon worked, the profiles of the people who were infected gave us the proof we needed," Soper explained. "You see, the wealthy are generally protected from being infected by their cooks since cooks almost never handle raw food. In most wealthy households, the footmen, waitresses or butlers prepare salads for the family. They place the garnishes on the meats and vegetables. They cut the bread. Cooks handle cooked food for the families, which is the origin of the title cook.

"Of course, sometimes that protection fails. For example, Mary made ice cream with fresh peaches that all the Charles Henry Warren family and the staff, specifically remember eating. Heat kills typhoid, cold doesn't. Her handling of the fresh peaches provided the vector for the infection."

"It was once thought that the Hudson River ice was the cause of Typhoid Fever, isn't that true, Dr. Soper?" Smith asked

"Yes, Hudson River ice and a great many other things. However, while they do convey typhoid, they are the secondary cause of infection. The primary cause is the human carrier whose fecal matter infects the ice, milk or water source," Soper explained. "Once again this is an example of how cold does not kill the bacillus."

"Did Mary handle uncooked food for other people?" Smith asked.

"Yes she did," Soper went on. "While Mary did not handle the raw food that the family ate, she handled all the salads and breads for the help. If you look at the profile of the cases in households where Mary has cooked," he gestured to a large graph of the victims of typhoid from the households at which Mary had been employed, "Most of the patients come from the servant's quarters. In those households where typhoid was caught by the family, Mary was either the sole servant in the house at the time, or she prepared a particular food with raw fruits or vegetables in it or the infections were secondary to the ones she caused in the servants quarters.

"It was this profile, which led us – during the course of our investigation – to eliminate all the possible sources of typhoid except the cook. The test data from Dr. Park was merely confirmation of what we already suspected. We were able to isolate and identify Mary Mallon as the source of infection well before we actually had her in custody."

For the rest of the day Smith interrogated the members of the team that had conducted the investigation which had started with the outbreak in Oyster Bay. Finally Smith said, "The Department of Health rests, Your Honor."

O'Neill began his argument with the treatment of Mary Mallon by the police in their violent arrest and man handling of the woman, of the repeated violation of his client by running invasive tests without her permission and finally her incarceration in solitary confinement on North Brother Island because, in point of fact, she was the only typhoid carrier to be held in quarantine even though there were at this time other known carriers who had infected and killed more people in the course of their food handling than Mary had.

Finally he called Mary.

"I never in me life had the typhoid," Mary said. "I would know about it if I'd had it wouldn't I?"

"Mary, have you ever infected anyone?" O'Neill asked.

"Good Lord, it's the last thing that I would do," Mary said. Her face saddened at the idea. "Indeed I was so concerned that even before the Department of Health came and took me I had meself tested by Ferguson Laboratories at me own expense. They found nothin'. Six times they tested me and six times they found nothin'."

The hearing took a day. At the end of the summaries Judge Erlanger asked, "Have you anything to add, Mr. O'Neill?"

"Nothing, your Honor, except to state that I seek Mary Mallon's immediate release on the grounds of habeas corpus," O'Neill replied.

"I won't grant you that, Mr. O'Neill," Erlanger replied, gathering his papers and preparing to leave the court. "But I will take this matter under immediate advisement and you will hear from me very soon."

"All rise," the Bailiff called.

Everyone in the room rose as the Judge exited. There was an immediate buzz of conversation over the sounds of people exiting.

"You were brilliant, Mr. O'Neill," Mary said, eyeing the Bailiff who was moving toward her, ready to return her to the officers who would bring her back to North Brother island.

"Thank you, Mary," O'Neill smiled confidently.

"What do ya' think?" Mary asked.

"Hearings are funny things, Mary," O'Neill cautioned. "They're impossible to predict. But we have a better than even chance."

"I thought the judge looked sympathetic," Mary said, trying to find a positive answer.

"Time will tell, Mary. Time will tell."

Behind O'Neill Hal made eye contact. She smiled at him and then turned away.

The Bailiff moved forward, grabbed her arm and led her away toward the back of the room. When she reached the door she turned once more for one last glimpse of Hal.

Chapter 36

Waiting

In her tiny cottage on North Brother Island Mary was restless. Most days she could be found pacing the floor.

"I'm wearin' out the damned carpet," she muttered to herself. "No one to talk to. Nothin' to do. I'm sick of readin'."

She smiled at Lucky, who followed her every motion with his liquid brown eyes. Reaching down she scratched his chest, "I wish ya' could talk, Lucky. I'm goin' crazy in here by meself. Oh, that doesn't say anythin' about you, you're good company as far as ya' go. But, I can't stand the waitin' Lucky. It was easier when there was no hope."

Chapter 37

Soper and Baker Waiting

In George Soper's office at the New York Department of Health, Soper and Baker were examining a report from a typhoid outbreak in Portchester, New York.

"The source of contamination was standing there in the dairy big as life," Baker said, grinning at Soper. "He'd been working there for three weeks."

"Better than three months, I suppose," Soper said. "Did they fire him?"

"Actually, they moved him to a job on the grounds. Somewhere he can't come in contact with the milk," Baker replied. "I was very impressed with the fact that they did that."

Baker looked out the window for a moment, her eyes losing focus as she became lost in thought.

"It's a shame, you know," she said at last.

"What's a shame?" Soper asked, even as his eyes still scanned the report she had written.

"That Mary will never understand the contribution she's made. Without her we'd have had to close the dairy down, put dozens of people out of work," Baker replied. "Now we simply move one man."

"They're two sides of a thin coin – triumph and tragedy. I'm glad our side was triumphant. At least I hope our side is triumphant," Soper said, completely preoccupied with the report.

"Do you think they'll ever let her go?" Baker asked.

"I hope not," Soper replied.

"But Dr. Soper, she hasn't done anything wrong. We're not locking up people like Fred Moersch and he's infected far more people than Mary has."

"He has a family to support."

"So we're keeping her in isolation because she's a single woman?"

"She's not clean," Dr. Baker.

"What do you mean she's not clean?"

"You know these Irish. Their slums are teeming with disease," Soper said. "Just last week we took thirty people to North Brother Island because they were spreading tuberculosis."

"But typhoid and tuberculosis aren't the same thing. They are not spread in the same way. If Mary took other work, the way Fred Moersch has, why couldn't she leave? We found the alternative work for him, why can't we find it for her?"

"Good gracious, Dr. Baker," Soper said, impatience in his voice. "You're beginning to sound like a social worker."

"I just think it's a shame that she has to live out there in isolation because she's the only person who has any relation to typhoid on the entire island. We are not being even handed," Baker snapped, picking up a new report and ending the conversation.

Chapter 38

The Decision

On her second visit to the Tweed Courthouse, Mary was not quite as impressed as she had been the first time; more anxious perhaps, but much less impressed.

As Hal followed Mary and O'Neill up wrought iron stairs to the second floor, he chided her for chewing on a hang nail.

"You're lettin' the whole world know how nervous you are," he told her under his breath.

"I've got every reason in that world for bein' nervous," she retorted, biting harder and drawing blood. "Damn!"

"Told ya' so," he said with a twinkle in his eye.

"Arse hole," she muttered angrily.

"Be careful Mary, these people don't like women soundin' like teamsters, they'll use it agin' ya'." Hal whispered, taking his clue from O'Neill's look of horror.

As they neared room 202 they saw the group from the Department of Health entering the courtroom ahead of them. The look on Mary's face is pure murder.

"All rise. Hear ye, hear ye. All those having business before this Supreme Court of the State of New York step forward and you shall be heard," the Bailiff cried.

Judge Mitchell Erlanger entered once again from a door behind the bench and took his seat.

"Mr. O'Neill, Mr. Smith. As you both know, it is not necessary for me to hold a session of the Court in order to hand down my decision," the Judge instructed. "However, on the matter of the New York Department of Health versus Mary Mallon, I wanted to make certain that all of you heard and understood my findings completely. I particularly wanted Mary Mallon and the representatives of the New York Department of Health to hear what I have to say.

"As you so eloquently argued, Mr. O'Neill, Mary Mallon has committed no crime, did not receive representation by counsel and did not receive even a hint of the due process granted her under the United States Constitution. All that was very wrong. I am particularly distressed by Mary Mallon's isolation on North Brother Island and I intend to see that such treatment is rectified to some extent.

"I want to make it absolutely clear to the New York Department of Health that such a miscarriage of justice will not be tolerated in the future. We have Courts and we have laws and in a country of law the law must be trusted to do the right thing. Do you understand gentlemen?"

Mary's eyes swam with joy as she listened to the court inform her tormentors that they were wrong in the way they had treated her. She knew with certainty that she was going to win this case and be free to restart her life. Perhaps somewhere other than the city, where the Department of Health had destroyed her reputation, but somewhere where her cooking would be appreciated and she could prove herself again.

"But, even as the Court disagrees with the Departments methods," Erlanger continued, "The Court must agree with Mr. Smith in citing the imminent-peril section of New York's City Charter and the health laws of the State of New York. So, while the Court deeply sympathizes with this unfortunate woman, it must protect the community against a recurrence of the spreading of this disease. I therefore remand Mary Mallon to the custody of the Bailiff and instruct that she be returned to North Brother Island until such time as all questions of her medical condition have been resolved."

Mary jumped to her feet, "No!"

The Bailiffs stepped forward and took her arms.

She struggled fiercely, kicking and elbowing the hapless Bailiffs. Within seconds they were joined by three officers who had been standing by in case of just such an event. "You can't. It's not fair."

The officers dragged her out of court as flash bulbs popped. Mary struggled, fought, punched and snarled. Her last view of the court was of George Soper's look of satisfaction.

She was so enraged she did not hear O'Neill calling to her, "We'll fight it, Mary. Don't worry. We won't stop here."

Standing beside George Soper, Josephine Baker looked grim.

"Some days there's certainly no joy in the law," Erlanger muttered to himself, as he stood to exit the courtroom.

Chapter 39

Wrongful Imprisonment Suit

Mary and George Francis O'Neill were found strolling together along the south shore of North Brother Island. They walked past the burned out remains of the sidewheeler The General Slocum, on to Mary's favorite group of rocks on the west side of the island from which she could gaze at the Bronx, across the East River.

"Did you read in the paper that they're addin' chlorine to the water supply for the whole city?" Mary asked. "Ya' get interested in such things when you're in my position; 1909 and so much progress. Just think of it, man can fly, and I'm still a hazard to the public health."

"I've filed a lawsuit for damages resulting from wrongful imprisonment," O'Neill said, interrupting the small talk.

"How much?" Mary asked, fixing him with a penetrating stare.

"Fifty thousand dollars," O'Neill grinned at her expecting her to be delighted. "You'll read about it in the papers tomorrow."

"It's not enough," Mary responded, a look of deepest anger furrowing her brow.

"It's a fortune, Mary," O'Neill replied. "You wouldn't make that if you cooked for the next 40 years."

"It's my life George Francis," Mary flashed. "I want the city to pay for lockin' me away here, for the solitary confinement that nearly drove me mad, for destroyin' me reputation and turnin' me into a person no one would have in their home let alone their kitchen."

"It's not so bad here," O'Neill comforted. "And they've stopped the isolation. You have friends now."

"You mean now that they're lettin' me work in the laundry instead of keepin' me in solitary it's not so bad?" Mary retorted. "Life in prison is life in prison no matter how you dress it up. You know, out there in the real world it's a very risky place. Do you have a job? Can you get a job? Will the job pay enough? Can you keep your health so you can do the work? Will a runaway come along and trample you to death? But at least you know you're alive out there. I want... no, I need to get out. I need to breathe the free, fresh air of risk."

"Enough to agree to whatever demands the Board of Health puts on you?" O'Neill asked, looking at her out of the side of his eye.

"What do ya' mean?" Mary asked, stopping dead in her tracks.

"Did you follow last month's elections?" O'Neill asked. There was something in his voice that told Mary that he had some real news for her, if he would ever get around to mentioning it.

"Of course. I do read the papers, ya' know," Mary replied, holding down her temper in the knowledge that it would do no good to alienate her one champion.

"There's a new administration in City Hall, Mary," O'Neill explained. "A whole new set of politicians out to prove the old set wrong. These are men who won't remember issuing warrants for your arrest or appearing in court against you. Scuttlebutt has it that the new people in the Department of Health think that you have been wronged. I think this would be a very good time to appeal to the Department of Health for release from this hospital."

"Ya' mean beg 'em?" Mary asked defiance standing plain in her throat.

O'Neill ignored her anger. "There's a chance, just a chance mind you, that if we play it right, these men will let you out. Are you willing to agree to what they want?"

"I won't let them cut me up," Mary said. "Killin' me on the operating table would be a grand solution to their problem, now wouldn't it."

"I don't think an operation will be necessary. I really do think they want to let you out because it's the right thing to do. Even if they want to let you out to make the other party look bad, you'll be out just the same," O'Neill said.

"I'll hate it, knucklin' under to them. It's like pleadin' guilty to a crime you didn't commit," Mary said at last.

"That's not my question, Mary," O'Neill said. "They're going to make demands on you, particularly with regard to handling food, are you willing to work at another profession if that is the price of freedom?"

"Yes," Mary said after awhile. "If I don't have to have the operation, yes."

Chapter 40

New York Department of Health

In the conference room, Charles Darlington sat at the head of the table. George Soper and Josephine Baker sat to his right. Mary and O'Neill sat on his left. With all his heart Darlington wished he had not invited Soper. The looks between Mary and Soper were so rife with dislike that he despaired of carrying off the meeting without violence. At the far end of the table sat a court reporter, with his numerous sharpened pencils and pads, prepared to take the conversation down in short hand.

"Do you understand that we are discussing the terms of your release, Mrs. Mallon?" Charles Darlington asked, addressing Mary.

Mary nodded but sullenly chose not to say anything.

"They are releasing her against my very strong advice," Soper whispered to Baker, the anger standing plain in his voice. "Look at her, she's still resisting."

"Can you blame her, Dr. Soper," Baker said. "She's been held in solitary for two years, and she still believes that her tests are negative."

"Well, 73% of them are positive, she's no innocent," Soper whispered back.

"We can't keep her locked up forever," Baker whispered back. "It makes us look bad."

"Imagine how we'll look when she goes out and kills a few more of our most important citizens," Soper replied.

"You must answer my questions with a yes or no, Mrs. Mallon, because this conversation is being taken down by a court reporter and he needs to hear your answer. Do you understand that we are discussing the terms of your release?" Darlington repeated.

"Yes," Mary replied, speaking between her teeth.

"Do you understand that your release is to be conditional?" Darlington asked.

"Yes."

"Do you understand that if you violate even one of the terms of your release that you will be returned to North Brother Island?" Darlington asked, checking off each yes response on his list.

"Yes," Mary clenched her teeth to bite back the rage she felt at being threatened like a common criminal.

"The first condition to which you have agreed is that you will never again cook for any member of the general public, privately or publicly," Darlington looked up from the paper. "Do you agree?"

"Yes," Mary said.

"You have read the guidelines for living with typhoid in my presence. Do you agree?" Darlington droned, going down the list.

"Yes," Mary replied.

"Did you understand those guidelines?" Soper interjected.

Mary refused to answer him.

"Did you understand them?" Darlington asked.

"Yes," Mary fairly spat the word.

"And you agree to abide by them?" he asked.

"Yes," Mary hissed, glowering at Soper.

"Would you sign the bottom of the sheet for me?" Darlington asked.

Mary took the offered pen and signed the document in her distinctive, well-rounded, schoolgirl penmanship.

"One final condition, Mrs. Mallon," Darlington said, blotting the ink on the document that she had just signed.

"Yes?" Mary asked, looking him directly in the eyes for the first time all afternoon.

"You absolutely must report to this office on the third Tuesday of every month." Darlington looked right at Mary before asking, "Is that understood?"

"Yes," Mary agreed. Her lips were tight, her jaw clenched.

"Very well then," Darlington said, relaxing back in his chair. He pushed an envelope toward her. Here is $200.00 payment for your work in the Hospital laundry we subtracted the expenses for your upkeep these past three years."

"Thank you," Mary managed, looking at the paltry sum that represented more than two years of her life – years in which so many bad things had happened. Hal taking in housemates to meet the rent that she had not been able to earn. Once they had shared an apartment together, now she could no longer call her home her own.

Years in which she nearly went mad with the loneliness of the cottage by the river. Years when she saw no one but Lucky for days on end. Years in which the career she had built so carefully since she was fifteen had been destroyed by the publicity her case had received. Years that should have brought nearly $4000 into her coffer, marked off by a $200 pittance and the chance to earn half of what she was worth staring her in the face.

Mary glared at Soper as she and O'Neill stood to leave.

Mary didn't say a word until she and O'Neill had actually walked through the courthouse doors.

"I can't believe I'm free," she said at last. Her superstitious nature cautioned her against risking a celebration too early. Don't tempt fate she had always been told.

"Next step is our lawsuit," O'Neill said, smiling at her. He was a little disappointed that she wasn't more excited.

"How can I ever pay you, Mr. O'Neill?" Mary asked, holding the dollars Darlington had given her tight in her fist. She did not want to give him the money, but her strong sense of integrity forced her hand forward. "Here. A down payment on the bill."

"No Mary, that's yours to start your new life with," O'Neill said, pushing her hand back toward her. "I've told you that I'm being paid by the Hearst Newspapers. I'll be in touch."

"Thank you," Mary replied, pushing the bills into her purse.

She turned and walked away from him, headed toward the corner. Hal was there across the street waiting for her. He was leaning casually against the building holding Lucky on a leash, his cap perched jauntily over his right eye. Mary extended her mannish stride as she rushed toward him. When she reached him they kissed briefly and he enfolded her with his arm, clipping her around her broad waist. They did not look back as they walked down the street toward their new future.

Chapter 41
Sarah Josephine Baker

Josephine Baker was busy. She and a group of nurses, working in the slums of Manhattan, had started to train young mothers in how to care for their babies. Although it was generally assumed that mothering was an innate skill, Baker had discovered that much of the high infant mortality in the city was caused by ignorance. She and her nurses started with the basics, how to clothe infants to keep them from getting too hot, how to feed them a good diet, how to keep them from suffocating and how to keep them clean and diaper rash free.

Armed with the new Pure Food and Drug Act, she set up a new system to assure that all milk that was sold in the city was pasteurized, uncontaminated and did not contain additives like contaminated water and chalk to thin them out. She had also invented an infant formula made out of water, calcium carbonate, lactose, and cows' milk, which enabled mothers to go to work so that they could support their families.

Now, in addition to tracking typhoid epidemics, she had started the Little Mothers League to train older sisters to care for their younger siblings. She had also started working on a means of preventing blindness – that was caused by gonorrhea – in infants. She found time in her busy schedule to lead the campaign to make sure every school in the city was given its own in-house doctor and nurse, so that children could be routinely checked for diseases like lice and trachoma.

Even with this carving out of her own area of influence, typhoid was still a passion and following what happened to Mary Mallon continued to hold her interest. She did not for a minute believe that Mary, who had been inordinately healthy her whole life, understood that she was a typhoid carrier. She didn't believe that the Department of Health had adequately explained hygiene to Mary. More than that, she believed that Mary had been treated unfairly.

In addition to the infamous confectioner Fred Moersch, whom the city supported as a plumber's assistant, several new healthy typhoid carriers had come across her desk. Tony Labella, blamed for infecting 122 people five of whom had died, had been isolated on North Brother Island for a mere two weeks before his release. Alphonse Cotils, a restaurant and bakery owner, had been identified as the cause of a severe outbreak, and had signed an agreement similar to the one Mary had signed agreeing not to prepare food for other people. Cotils had been found back at work in his restaurant only weeks after his release.

As a professional woman in a man's world, Baker understood the prejudice against Mary. Woman had not yet been granted the vote and there were decided limits on their ability to enter into contractual agreements. At a time when boarding houses' signs read, 'Jews, Negros and Irish need not apply,' and working women, particularly in the domestic servant class were looked down upon. The fact that Mary did not have a family, and was not considered a "bread earner," weighed heavily against her. But beyond that, Baker wrote in the notes for her future book, Mary's Irish temper and occasional foul mouth, plus the fact that she fought so hard against her incarceration and refused to accept the fact of her carrier status, worked against her.

All the social elements were nothing compared to Mary's success as a cook for the wealthy. Baker realized that when Selina Bowen, daughter of one of New York's most prestigious families, died, Mary's imprisonment was guaranteed. She had to be kept away from the families of the rich and powerful and the fact that the hiring practices of the day were so loose made it necessary to protect them from Mary by keeping track of her by incarceration.

Baker removed her rimless glasses and rubbed her tired eyes. Even with all her understanding of Mary, and the system in which the poor woman found herself, she could not find a way to help her. She could understand her, but Mary was one person and she could not jeopardize the thousands she was helping to defend a woman who would not comply with the system in order to help herself.

Chapter 42

Life Without Cooking

Mary Mallon struggled across the teeming street balancing a huge basket of laundry on her shoulder. The smell, the filth and noise assaulted her as she wove through the traffic that clogged Broadway. The city was baking in a heat wave. The air was so hot and humid that she wasn't certain if she was inside her body or outside of it. Sweat ran down her neck into the dark shirtwaist she habitually wore. It seeped through at the breast, back and waist making her clothes so damp that she could have rung them out and filled a bowl with water. The skin under her great breasts and between her heavy thighs burned from heat rash.

Panting, she climbed the steps to the front door. She balanced the basket against the wall beside the door, fetched her key from her dress pocket and unlocked the front door. She struggled to keep the heavy door open and move the huge basket inside without spilling the clothes.

In the hall, Mary put down the basket and relocked the door. She picked up the basket and, carrying it before her, struggled up the first flight of stairs. The stairs were narrow and Mary had to turn the basket with the narrow end leading the way so that it could pass between the banister and the wall. It made the load heavier and far more awkward. She reached the first landing panting, rested for a few minutes and then proceeded with her struggle to the third floor.

When she reached the third floor landing, she balanced the basket against the door while she struggled with the key. She was, if possible, hotter, redder and sweatier than she had been in the street.

As she let herself into the kitchen, she was immediately greeted by an ecstatic Lucky who jumped on her, wildly wagging his tail as if to show her exactly how much he loved her and had missed her.

"Down, Lucky, down," she said. "You'll like to bowl me over. Sit."

Lucky lowered his front paws and sat. She knelt before him, taking his soft ears in her big hands and rubbing them between her fingers.

"There's a good boy," she said lovingly. She had developed the habit of talking to the dog during the lonely years of solitary confinement and she kept it up as if he was having chats with her. Hal found it funny, and teased her about it, but she didn't change. The conversations with Lucky had saved her sanity and she knew it.

After giving Lucky his due, she stood and placed the laundry basket on the kitchen table. Then she turned and reached for Lucky's leash, prattling to him as she prepared to leave the house.

"I'll take ya' out for a walk before I get started. God, it's hot in here and going to be hotter when I have to warm those irons with the boilin' water. Still, things could be worse I suppose. We could still be using the old coal stoves to heat the irons. Now that would be hot. And I could be luggin' the water up all those stairs too. These are fine times we're livin' in, Lucky."

The door closed behind her, she locked it again and she and Lucky clattered down the four flights of stairs to the ground floor.

Mary and Lucky walked and shopped. Her shopping had changed since her return from North Brother Island. She made do with more potato. She bought a small amount of milk, measured into a container, butter, two onions and a pound of kale to go with the potato. She walked past the butcher shop with a nostalgic look for the old days when her stews had been built around meat.

"Like the old days in Ireland," she complained under her breath thinking back to the reason she had been driven to immigrate. She well remembered the stark poverty that had brought her here, where she had done so well for herself until she had met George Soper.

When she had bought her few groceries and made sure of Lucky's needs – adding to the filth of the streets – she went back home, climbing the stairs again to the sweltering, airless rooms that the sun had beaten upon all day.

She released Lucky from his leash and walked to the sink in the corner. There she filled a bowl with water for the dog before filling four large pots that she put on the gas stove to heat. As the water heated, she cut up the potatoes and dumped them unceremoniously into the fourth of the pots that were heating on the stove.

Next she cut the kale, removing the large stems and slicing into the greens until they were reduced to small pieces. Finally she diced the onion and set it to the side.

"I'm making colcannon, Lucky, like I did in the old country," Mary informed the panting shepherd, who lay near her feet. The dog liked to be where she was, and never let her out of his sight when she was in the house. "It's so famous in the old country that they wrote a song about it."

Mary's voice was tuneless as she sang,

"Did you ever eat Colcannon, made from lovely pickled cream?

"With the greens and scallions mingled like a picture in a dream.

"Did you ever make a hole on top to hold the melting flake

"Of the creamy, flavored butter that your mother used to make?

"Yes you did, so you did, so did he and so did I.

"And the more I think about it sure the nearer I'm to cry.

"Oh, wasn't it the happy days when troubles we had not,

"And our mothers made Colcannon in the little skillet pot."

She separated the laundry into white and colored batches. Within the colored pile she separated each color into individual groupings. She washed the colored clothing first because washing the whites was such a process. Next, she removed one of the pots of boiling water from the stove, ran some cold water into the sink and poured the boiling water into the sink to heat the cold. She refilled the pot and set it back on the stove to heat.

For the next half hour, as the potatoes simmered on the back of the stove, she scrubbed the laundry item by item against the corrugations on the rectangular washing board. The harsh lye soap had brought chilblains to her hands; which were red, cracked and ulcerating. Despite the pain of her irritated hands, she kept scrubbing each garment, dipping and scrubbing until she thought they must be clean. Each piece was then wrung out and placed on the drain board. When she had finished with a color she drained the sink, refilled it, poured another pot of hot water into it and began the rinsing process.

"Who would suppose the likes of me would be makin' do in an apartment with runnin' water and a gas stove?" she said to Lucky who wagged his tail at the attention. "It's a proper luxury even if the water's cold."

When she had rinsed each item of colored cloth, she hung the clothing on a line that stretched from the back of her apartment, to the back of a building across the alley. Hal had strung six of these clothes lines each of which was moved along through a pulley. She used them daily.

"I don't know what I like best, not havin' to lug the water up four flights of stairs or not havin' to share space with a coal burnin' stove. It's bad enough with the gas. Imagine how we'd be if I had to heat the water with coal," she said, looking at Lucky who panted happily. His mouth turned up at the corners as if he was smiling.

She checked on the potatoes with a carving fork and, finding them cooked through, removed them from the heat and poured them into a colander to drain. She cleaned off the potato residue and then filled the pot with water again but did not place the pot on the stove, because she knew she would need the burner. Finally she turned on the oven to preheat it.

She pulled forward one of the pots that was already boiling, pushed the chopped Kale into a metal strainer and set the strainer over the boiling water to steam. While it steamed she took one of her great iron frying pans, threw a tablespoon of butter into it and, placed it on a burner. When the butter had melted, she poured the diced onion into the pan and, stirred rapidly, until the onion was translucent. She removed the onion and the kale from the heat, replaced the water in the pot and continued to boil water for washing.

At the kitchen table which sat over the bath tub in the center of the room, she mashed the cooked potatoes, added the kale and onion and stirred the mixture together. Finally she greased a baking pan, poured the colcannon mixture into it, placed half the butter in little cubes over the top of it and set it into the preheated oven.

While the colcannon baked, she resumed her washing. This time she added Mrs. Stewarts Bluing to one of the large pots to whiten the whites then started the process all over again. She scrubbed until the ring around the collar, or the deeply stained hems were visibly clean, wringing, rinsing, wringing and finally pushing the white material into the pot of bluing. There was one more step for collars and shirts, and that was starching, which she handled once the clothes were a brilliant white.

"You wouldn't have been readin' it in the paper, Lucky," she chattered as she worked. "But they've started to pasteurize the milk for this city, whatever that means. They say it'll kill germs. Between them chlorinatin' the water and pasteurizin' the milk there's hope for me yet."

Using long tongs, she lifted a shirt out of the bluing and transferred it to a pot that contained liquid starch.

"Oh, and what a fuss there was," she laughed. "People protestin' that the government was out to kill them by destroyin' their food. You know what I think, Lucky? I think nobody knows anything. They got their pet theories of course. I know all about theories ya' know, theories are what they use to persecute people like me – and then they spend a lot of time and money makin' themselves right. And everyone says 'Oh how brilliant they are,' and they don't care who they destroy in the process."

It was a long day. The clothes were cleaned and hung to dry ready for ironing with the hot water-filled irons in the morning. When she was finished, she took Lucky for another walk. On the way back she picked up two rolls at the local bakery.

At the end of the week Mary returned from walking Lucky when she found Hal sitting at the kitchen table drinking a beer.

"You're back then," she said by way of greeting.

"Is that any way to say hello to the man you haven't seen all week?" Hal laughed.

She walked over to give him a peck on the cheek but he pulled her onto his lap and pressed his mouth against hers. She pulled back in a temper.

"Look at this," she said, pulling six bills out of her pocket and thrusting the money at his face as if he had something to do with it. "This is me pay for sixteen hours of sweatin' over a hot iron all day."

"Enough for a noggin," Hal said, taking a nip at her neck.

"I used to be a cook," Mary said, her bitterness audible. "I used to earn $24.00 a week. Now look at me. I've joined the legions of the workin' poor. I work sixteen hours a day for the pleasure of gettin' behind in me bills."

"Quit belly achin' Mary. I like havin' ya' here and that's a fact," Hall said, clearly showing the love he had for her with the passion in his eyes. "We aren't doin' so bad."

"I don't like bein' dependent, Hal. Even though you're the best man I've ever known," she said. "I'll see if I can find a different job, somethin' where the pay's a little better. I don't mind the hard work, mind ya', I've worked hard all me life. It's the pay I mind."

Chapter 43
Lawsuit Discussed

George O'Neill's office was dominated by his roll top desk. The office was covered with wainscot to the height of the chair tops to protect the white plaster on the walls from chair damage. O'Neill welcomed Mary as if greeting an old friend.

"Welcome Mary," he said showing her to one of four ladderback chairs that surrounded his small conference table. "It's good to see you."

"I don't mean to trouble you," Mary apologized, "but I wanted to know what's happenin' with the lawsuit?"

"It takes time, Mary," O'Neill said, making his own apology. "The law moves very slowly."

"You've heard nothin' then," she asked. "Ya' see gettin' along without cookin' is hard. I run out of money before I run out of week. I know these people at the Department of Health think that all domestic service is the same, but it isn't. It isn't at all."

"With these kinds of actions, the government has to agree to hear suits against itself before we can get into court. It's a little tricky sometimes," O'Neill explained.

"Do you think there's a chance?" Mary asked, and O'Neill heard a shade of desperation in her voice.

"There are so many questions about your case that I'm sure there's a chance," O'Neill hastened to reassure her. "Just have faith, Mary. We'll prevail."

"Mr. O'Neill, I came here when I was fifteen from a village hardly worthy of the name. I came by meself because there wasn't a chance in Hell of me makin' anythin' of me life at home. I learned early on that the best payin' job in the area of domestic service was cookin' and I worked like a dog to get to the top of that field. The

Department of Health has taken all those years away from me, half me life, and replaced them with nothin'. I want them to pay for what they took."

"Patience Mary, that's all I can tell you. I'm doing my best. It takes time."

"I'll be back then," Mary said bitterly.

Chapter 44

The Way Down

Mary was on her hands and knees scrubbing the floor with a brush and soapy water, each brush stroke reflecting her deep and abiding anger.

Later in the day she took her frustration out on the oriental rugs. She hung them on a clothes line and attacked them with a rug beater. No one who did not know Mary would have realized that she was in a towering rage and that the rugs were bearing the cost.

"I used to be a cook and have some pride in what I did," she muttered to herself punctuating each word with a hearty swat against the rug.

Even emptying the dustbin into the trash was a statement of rage. It seemed to Mary that everything she did was punishment for a crime she had never committed.

"I didn't like doin' this when I was just doin' it for meself," she observed with wry amusement. "How is it that I've been brought so low?"

Pay was handed out at the end of the week by the butler. Mary gazed at the few bills and coins in her hands. Under the glow of the gaslight her face was twisted with disappointment.

Hal tried to make a joke of her rage. He held up the paper which he enjoyed reading from cover to cover, "Well, you're stuck now," he announced with a great twinkle in his eye.

"And why am I stuck, pray tell?" Mary flashed with the temper that he loved so much.

"They just passed the Mann Act, no more crossin' state lines for illicit purposes. Ya' missed out," Hal laughed.

"Oh you're so full of it," Mary said, trying to suppress her own laughter. "Who the hell would want to use me as a prostitute?"

Hal lifted his eyebrows up and down in a suggestive leer and reached his hands out in her direction. "Oh, me darlin' I would use you as a prostitute or any other kind of 'tute any day of the week. Come here. Let's practice turnin' ya into a woman of sin."

"You're incorrigible Hal," she laughed. Hal's appetite for her was the single bright spot in her life and she sent a quick prayer of gratitude for it before she collapsed in his arms.

Chapter 45

The World of Risk

Mary staggered along the snow-covered sidewalk, a full basket of freshly washed and ironed laundry. Near the corner was a wide spot where water had dripped from a roof gutter. Under the snow, the sidewalk was covered with black ice.

Mary's boot caught the ice and her foot went out from under her. She dropped the hamper, scattering the freshly washed clothes across the filthy wetness of the sidewalk and caught herself with her hand. The full weight of her body snapped both bones at the wrist. She rocked in pain, folding her body around her right arm.

"Oh God. Oh God," she moaned, as bile rose to her throat.

"You all right, miss?" the shop owner said, rushing out to help her, worry creasing his wrinkled face.

"I think I broke me arm," Mary managed. The pain was so intense she could barely speak.

"There's a doctor on the next street. Come, give me your hand let me help you up. Do ya' feel like you can walk there?" the shop owner asked.

"Can I pick up the laundry and leave it in your shop?" Mary asked, fighting the feeling that she would vomit at any second. "It wouldn't do to be losin' it now." She didn't know which made her sicker, the loss of the hours of washing and ironing or the pain of the broken bones grating against each other in her wrist.

Chapter 46

Where is the Bottom?

For Mary, working in the infamous Alphabet City of the lower east side was an almost unbearable step down. She and Hal had been forced to move from their luxurious tenement in Hell's Kitchen when Mary had lost her income following her fall. Now, in the most densely populated neighborhood in the city, she and Hal shared a one bedroom in a building in which five and six families shared apartments built for one.

In Hell's Kitchen she had walked in neighborhoods where Gaelic could be heard on every corner, now she washed floors for the Central European Jews and Italians who were poorer than she was, who lived in buildings with no running water and no indoor plumbing.

Her "fall from grace," as she often called it, did not bother her nearly as much as the way she had been treated after her accident. No credit had been given for the fact that the laundry had been washed and ironed. The only fault that had been found was that she would be unable to redo what had been soiled by her fall and, since she had not delivered all of it clean, she was not paid. Mary's anger smoldered like banked coal.

Mary had replaced her domestic service job with a manager's position in exchange for free rent. The building was filthy. The smell of urine permeated the halls. Tenants left garbage to rot. She herself was having problems with the pain in her arm. She could still mop floors if no one looked too closely. And no one in Alphabet City was apt to look. With her right arm in a splint and sling, Mary pushed the filthy mop gingerly along the even more filthy floor. She was unable to ring it out or rinse it, and soon she found herself pushing swirls of mud. Doing an imperfect job hurt her pride.

She spent most of her day in her small apartment – two rooms without the luxury of running water – resting and thinking about her life before the fall with the luxury of cold running water, a bath and a toilet. In this new building everyone used an outhouse in the back yard to do their business and carried chamber pots from their apartments down during the day.

The outhouse had two sections, one for men and one for women. Each section had two seats, so people could do their business in pairs. There was no privacy, and the smell was unbearable.

Since all water had to be carried upstairs, it was never used for bathing – the buildings contained no sinks, drains, toilets or bathtubs. Ice boxes, and the ice to keep them cool, was a luxury for people who were less poor than those who lived in this neighborhood, so food had to be purchased every day. The primary bathing location for residents in the northern half of the area was the Asser Levy bath house on 23rd Street and Avenue C, five blocks from Mary's building.

Mary and Hal talked endlessly about work opportunities in the city. Hal's work in construction was fairly steady even though it was dangerous and did not pay particularly well. Work for Mary was less steady and the pay was miserable.

It had been the Triangle Shirt Waist Fire in the Asch building at the corner of Washington Place and Greene Street that informed Mary's decision to return to cooking. Many of the 146 victims of the fire – girls who had been locked into the building on the eighth, ninth and tenth floors – were Jewish immigrants who lived in the neighborhood. Some of them had lived in Mary's building. As news of the fire leaked out anger and bitterness flooded the streets.

The exit doors had been locked to prevent the girls from leaving early. The horse drawn fire truck ladders and hoses only reached to the sixth floor, so neither water nor rescue were available to the young girls screaming for help above them. Human torches had leapt 100 feet to the street. It was the worst industrial disaster in the city to date. The neighborhood agreed, too many people looking for too few jobs allowed such atrocities to take place. The politicians had failed to pass laws to protect the workers because they had been bought and paid for by the business owners. Mary watched and listened and made decisions about her choices.

Chapter 47

Put That On My Tombstone

Mary could already see the news writ' large on George O'Neill's face.

"It's no good Mary," he said without preamble. "The government has not agreed to hear the case against itself."

"But they..." she stammered.

"They claim that by giving you a hearing in the New York Supreme Court and finding you in effect guilty, that justice was served and that the Department of Health was not in violation of the law," he said sadly. "In trying to help you one way, I've harmed you in another. I'm deeply sorry.

"I just can't win can I," Mary said, and it was as if there was a decision underlying her remark that O'Neill greatly feared, even as he thought it was justified. "Thank you Mr. O'Neill. Ya' did your best."

Mary turned toward the door, her broad shoulders straight, her body filled with a great dignity that O'Neill had never see in her before. Always he had seen her as bulky, unattractive and angry. Now he saw the strength of character that had pulled her by her Irish immigrant bootstraps from a child of fifteen to the top of her field in an unfriendly world where 'Irish need not apply' signs dotted the landscape.

"You did your best," he muttered, as the door closed behind her. "Put that on my tombstone."

Chapter 48

Decision

In their tiny one bedroom Manager's apartment in Alphabet City, Mary and Hal drank beer at the kitchen table. Lucky lay beside Mary resting his black muzzle on her bare foot. The newspapers, which were such a mainstay to Hal, were filled with the stories of the sinking of the Titanic and the dreadful stories of the Irish in steerage having been locked into the bowels of the ship and left to drown without a chance.

Hal and Mary had finished their meager supper and started drinking early. For Mary this was a new habit. Even though most cooks, and nearly all Irish, had a reputation for drunkenness she had abstained for most of her life. When Hal had teased her about it she had reminded him that the road up had been tough for her and she wasn't going to jeopardize it by drinking it away. When the Department of Health had robbed her of her profession she had started drinking.

"Jesus Mary, I can't stand it. They renamed me baseball team. They're callin' the Highlanders the Yankees. I just can't stand it," Hal said, staring miserably at his beer. Mary wasn't listening.

"To hell with justice," Mary said, raising her glass. Her words were a bit slurred though she wasn't so drunk that she didn't know what she was saying.

"I'll drink to that," Hal replied, tapping her glass with his. He was a little farther along than she was, having had a head start before she had returned from her meeting with O'Neill.

"To hell with the Department of Health," Mary toasted again, her face drawn in bitter, angry lines.

"I'll also drink to that," Hal said. He clinked his glass against hers again.

"To hell with *Mister* George Soper, the son-of-a-bitch pipe and drain expert," Mary ground on.

"I'll drink to him too," Hal said. For a man drinking to Mary's worst day in years, he sounded surprisingly happy.

"I've tried, Hal. You know I have," Mary said, putting down her glass and leaning toward him. Her voice was earnest, almost pleading. "But they make a decree and they don't tell you how you're goin' to feed yourself."

"You couldn't cook with that arm, Mary," Hal said, indicating the sling and the splint.

"No, but I'd have a little put by," Mary replied. "Look at us Hal, we used to have a splendid apartment in a good neighborhood. We used to have savin's. Now we're livin' in a one bedroom in Alphabet City and scrubbin' for people who have less than we have."

She stopped for a minute, her eyes taking on a distant look, her face growing pinched with anxiety.

"You don't think they're right, do you Hal?" she asked at last.

"What does it matter?" Hal asked, his voice earnest.

"Oh it matters, Hal. It matters. Because if they're right ya' see, if they're right, I gave the typhoid to Sean Mallon and me own darlin' Colleen. If they're right I killed me husband and my own child," Mary said, the agony standing clear in her words. "Oh Hal, they can't be right. It's beyond bearin'."

"What do they know? For goodness sake, Mary, every other word they said to you was 'maybe' and 'perhaps.' T'was the tainted water killed Sean Mallon and little Colleen, two out of the seven hundred that died. Here now. Dry your eyes. Have a sip. Now look at me. Remember that ya' saved the other one."

Tears started in Mary's eyes.

"Gave her away I did. Never to see her again," Mary said. Her throat was thick with grief. "I'm going back to cookin'. You're right Hal, I'll not be punished for a lot of maybes and perhapses. They can take their fookin' theories and shove 'em."

"That's my girl. I love it when ya' talk dirty," Hal said, pulling her off her chair and onto his lap. "Let's celebrate. Seems ta' me you'll be goin' away again so I might as well get as much as I can while you're here."

He kissed her lips and then licked away the tears that had dampened her cheeks. His hands were busy at the back of her dress undoing the buttons.

"God, Hal, what a gift you are to me," Mary sighed contentedly.

Chapter 49

Soper Observes

George Soper was sitting in his shirt sleeves and vest behind his great wooden desk reading a stack of reports when Josephine Baker entered shaking her umbrella.

"It's pouring outside," she said, flouncing her damp skirt to get whatever moisture she could off it before the dampness got absorbed by the heavy wool.

"My favorite weather," Soper grunted, as if defying her to take issue with his statement.

"There's no accounting for taste," Baker laughed.

"Don't get my carpets wet," Soper complained.

"She's disappeared you know," Baker said at last, collapsing into the big leather chair that sat beside his library.

"I warned them," Soper replied, a trace of anger making his voice brittle.

"Aren't you even going to ask me who disappeared?" Baker asked.

"It would be a redundancy. Mary Mallon was a disappearance waiting to happen," Soper retorted. He didn't bother to point out that Mary Mallon was the only "she" of any importance involved in typhoid who was immediately identifiable to any member of the Department of Health. Soper's specialty being typhoid, "she" was an obvious conclusion.

"Are those the typhoid reports from Gouvenier Hospital?" Baker asked. She was having less and less to do with typhoid as a result of her work with pregnant women and their babies, but everyone in the department had followed the outbreak at the hospital.

"Eight nurses and a woman clerk all stricken with typhoid," Soper said with a deep sigh. "What a mess. We've traced it to the water system. Why is it we always expect our hospitals to be free of disease?"

"How can they be free of disease, they're full of germs?" Baker asked. She was not following his train of thought. "Do they think it had anything to do with a food handler?"

"We're testing everyone who could possibly have come in contact with the water system so I doubt it was a food handler," Soper replied. "We have to figure out how it got into the system, however."

"So it wasn't Mary?" Baker said, relief coloring her voice.

"I don't think so, but I'm checking. I'm also checking to see if there are any kitchen staff who have left immediately after the outbreak, which is her pattern," Soper replied, his face grim.

"What do we do about her now that she's disappeared?" Baker asked.

"Follow the typhoid outbreaks until she makes a mistake," Soper replied.

"You think she'll go back to cooking?" Baker asked.

"Bound to. It's the only reason she would stop reporting to the Department of Health. Cooking is the only job she's trained for and one of the best paying jobs a woman can have, present company excluded. One day she'll kill one too many people. When she does, the disease will lead us to her. I nurture the secret fantasy that one of the people she cooks for will be one of those fine gentlemen from City Hall who so graciously let her off North Brother Island."

"You are a terror, George Soper," Baker replied. "But I do worry that she has gone back to cooking. Do you think she'll try to keep herself clean enough to protect those she cooks for."

"I suspect she'll try," Soper said. "But she won't succeed. It's an impossible task to keep herself clean enough in a cooking situation like that."

"I don't think she likes the idea of being a carrier," Baker mused.

"You're a romantic reading things into people to make them less villainous," Soper said.

"And you are a man who thinks that people who can't understand science are villains. There are hundreds of carriers in the city, George Soper, and Mary Mallon is the only one we've selected for quarantine, no not quarantine, isolation. We're as responsible as she is if she has failed to support herself and has gone back to cooking. She's right. We have persecuted her."

"She chose the wrong profession," Soper said, glowering resentfully at Baker. "You spend too much time looking after the interests of women to understand the interests of men."

"Lord, this case is laced with layers isn't it? Men against women, rich against poor and Mary in the middle," Baker said sadly, knowing that she could not save Mary no matter what she did. All she could do was repeat that Mary wasn't a criminal – and even that looked like a weak argument since Mary had disappeared.

Chapter 50

Atlantic City

Mary felt safe in the Marlborough House, one of the most talked about hotels on the boardwalk. It was famous for its liberal use of reinforced concrete which boasted Spanish and Moorish themes. The massive building was capped off with a signature dome and chimneys. The kitchen staff contributed to the Moorish theme by adding their famous paella, with locally caught shrimp and clams, to the menu.

Mary had never used saffron before nor had she strayed far from traditional roasts. The addition of a foreign dish to her repertoire opened a whole new world to her idea of cooking.

Among the hundreds in help that thronged the kitchens during the day, no one noticed Mary Edwards – except to remark that she was an extremely competent cook who worked hard and was generally liked.

In her off hours, Mary found Atlantic City enthralling. She had never been one to expose her light skin to the harsh sun and usually walked at times when the sun was rising or setting depending on her shift. She found the Victorian tourist site to be a beautiful city with its miles of world renowned herringbone boardwalk – a solution born of a need to eliminate the tracking in of sand that had once plagued the hotels that faced the beaches.

Her favorite spots to walk were along the salt marshes teeming with birds she had never seen before. Of all the things that Mary fell in love with in Atlantic City, saltwater taffy was her most favorite. She bought picture postcards, which were new to her, but did not send them to Hal in the fear that someone would trace her through her mail. She planned to bring him taffy and the postcards whenever she returned to New York.

In mid-August, more than a month after she had arrived, Mary returned from her early morning walk to find an ambulance parked behind the kitchen door. She stopped on the back delivery landing where Bertha, one of the morning cooks was watching as two attendants carried a loaded stretcher from the kitchen exit.

"Who would have thought it?" Bertha remarked. "Typhoid, here in Atlantic City. What's the world comin' to? People travelin' everywhere bringin' their diseases with them. It wasn't like this in the old days I'll tell ya'."

"Indeed," Mary muttered, cold fear gripping her stomach in a vise.

Chapter 51

Soper Tracking

George Soper preferred driving his Oldsmobile to riding on the train to Atlantic City. Life in the world of typhoid epidemics had grown dull since he had identified the cause of the disease. In the past, hundreds of people would have been infected, and an infected area would have been in stark panic. Now they simply removed the carrier and life went on as usual. The nature of his job had changed as well. Both because of Mary Mallon's disappearance, and because there were fewer and fewer outbreaks of typhoid, his job had spread to multiple areas well outside of New York City.

"I'd like to conduct a few tests on your cooking and food handling staff," Soper informed the manager, after his preliminary research had verified his suspicions that the Marlborough was the only hotel in Atlantic City to have suffered an outbreak.

"Those that are still here," the manager replied, in a tone designed to show his deep desire to cooperate in the investigation. He was frightened that his job would be on the line once the owners learned that typhoid had broken out on his watch. He worried that this Doctor from New York would blame him.

"People have left?" Soper asked. He had sped from his office and rushed down the coast as soon as the Department of Health had received notice of the outbreak. It could not have been more than two or three days since the first cleaning woman had been diagnosed with the disease.

"The day after the staff was informed of the outbreak, one of our cooks, Mary Edwards left," the manager said. "I thought it strange that any of the staff would leave in the middle of the season, but she asked for her pay and took the train the very next day."

"Has anyone else left?" Soper asked.

"No, as I said, it's the middle of the season. Resort hotels will generally have their staff in place by this time. She won't have an easy time getting summer work," the manager replied.

"Tell me, was she a large woman, very muscular and kind of mannish? Blond with remarkable blue eyes?" Soper asked.

"How did you know?" the manager asked, his voice filled with dread.

"I've been looking for Mary... Edwards did you say?" Soper responded.

"Yes, Edwards. Is there something I should have known about her that I missed in our interview?"

"Oh, you could not have known about her. She changed her name. Did you check her references?" Soper asked.

"We rarely do. We have so many in help here. If they don't work out we know it almost immediately and let them go," the manager said. "But who is this woman you have been looking for?"

"I strongly suspect that you have been visited by Mary Mallon," Soper said. "Typhoid Mary. I've been looking for her for a long time."

Chapter 52

Port Jefferson

Mary had returned to the North Shore of Long Island – though not to Oyster Bay. She had been searching the help wanted section of the *Times* and seen an ad for a small hotel in the picturesque village of Port Washington.

The hotel she had selected was small compared to the Marlborough House in Atlantic City, but she felt she could not be particular this late in the season.

Mary and the hotel owner were seated on either side of his large desk.

"These are excellent references Mrs. Brigham," he said as he replaced the written references into the envelope in which she kept them.

"Thank you, sir," Mary replied deferentially. She had not had to change the references in the slightest since every one of them referred to her as Mary – the prevailing disrespect for the servant class being what it was.

"How soon can you start?" he asked.

"It wouldn't trouble me to start right away," she responded. "Your advertisement said you needed someone immediately."

"Yes, I'm short staffed," he replied. "You can start right now if you're a mind to."

"I'll just be changin' into me uniform," she replied, rising from her chair.

Chapter 53

Baker and Jacobs

Josephine Baker and Inspector Joseph Jacobs were working companionably, examining slides in the third floor laboratory. Baker liked to drop by the lab to catch up on gossip in the world of epidemics and was always willing to pitch in while she was there.

"What do you think about this new income tax?" Jacobs asked, as he placed a new slide onto the microscope.

"I'm more interested in the new test for diphtheria immunity," Baker replied. "We are certainly living on the cutting edge of medicine and I love it."

"Speaking of cutting edges, did you see that new movie with Charlie Chaplin?" Jacobs asked.

"I love movies," Baker replied. "Do you think they'll introduce talking movies soon?"

"I'm willing to bet on it," Jacobs responded, turning the knob on the microscope to bring the slide into focus. "I see Dr. Soper's out of town again."

"Another possible sighting of Mary Mallon," Baker said. She had taken on the task of preparing the slides for Jacobs to examine and it required a bit of concentration. "Did you go over and take a look at the new Grand Central Terminal?"

"It's a work of art. I wouldn't like to be Mary Mallon if he ever catches up with her," Jacobs said, exchanging one slide for another after making notes on what he had seen on the first slide.

"The search is driving him crazy," Baker replied. "She's changed her clientele. She used to cook for wealthy families. Now she cooks for hotels. It's making it harder to find her. He always gets to the places she has infected days, sometimes hours, after she's left. She seems to have a sixth sense that he's coming."

"I doubt that. Seems to me that she left every place they've had an outbreak almost immediately afterward. Tell me something, Dr. Baker," Jacobs said looking up from the microscope. "Do think Dr. Soper's behavior is a little obsessive?"

"A little?" Baker laughed. "Yes, I'd say so. But it was that obsessive behavior that identified Mary Mallon and lead to the discovery that a-symptomatic humans could be typhoid carriers."

"What's it like working with him at a site?" Jacobs asked. Baker was the only person Jacobs knew who had accompanied Soper on an active investigation.

"Well, he certainly leaves no stone unturned," Baker replied. "I worked with him early in my career of course, and I found it highly instructive. It's one thing to learn about what to do when you're in school, or even when you're a resident. It's quite another thing to do it in the field with someone who is a true expert. You saw what he does when you were tracking her employment records. You can multiply by one hundred the attention to detail and the inspiration in the field."

"What do you think drives him?" Jacobs asked.

Baker laughed at the question. She had heard it before. "There was a rumor circulating that his childhood sweetheart died in a typhoid epidemic."

"Ahhhhhh," Jacob sighed, quite satisfied with the solution to his riddle.

"There is another rumor circulating that his sister died in a typhoid epidemic. Of course the rumor mongers might have confused his history with mine," Baker continued.

"Oh?" Jacobs asked.

"You do remember that I quit Vassar and entered medical school after my brother and father died of typhoid, don't you?" Baker asked, a sadness dimming her eyes.

"Identifying Mary as the first typhoid carrier has been very satisfying to me, even if I do believe we have not treated her well."

"I had forgotten about your family Dr. Baker," Jacobs said, embarrassment burning his cheeks.

"That's all right. It turned into a positive thing for me. I would never have discovered my passion for intervening in childbirth and early childhood mortality had I gone in the direction I was headed as a Vassar scholar," Baker soothed. "But let me continue, with Dr. Soper. There is a third rumor that Dr. Soper's entire family was wiped out by a typhoid epidemic which I think highly improbable given that typhoid only kills 10% of those it infects. That rumor includes the theory that the tragedy ruined his health. You can take your pick of any, or all of the rumors. I do not, however, personally know of a single person who actually has direct knowledge of any tragedy in his past that would justify his obsession."

"Severe arthritis isn't caused by typhoid," Jacobs said sounding confused by what she had just told him.

"Exactly," Baker agreed. "I personally subscribe to my own theory that obsession is Dr. Soper's way of doing things, nothing more complicated than that."

"A zealot?" Jacobs said.

"You might call him that," Baker replied. "I think of him as more of a medical Jesuit. Disease is his religion, and Mary Mallon happens to be his devil."

"That is a much kinder observation than the one that is floating around in the lab," Jacobs said.

"What observation is that?" Baker asked, looking sharply at the young inspector.

"That Mary was his ticket to fame," Jacobs said. "That it must be difficult for a man like him, who had built such a great reputation for ending huge epidemics to suddenly find himself with no more epidemics to handle. He was a hero in Ithaca and Watertown and now the rug has been pulled out from under him. All he has is Mary."

Baker frowned, not liking what she was hearing, although not greatly surprised by it. "Discovering the first typhoid carrier should be enough of a success in any life, Mr. Jacobs."

"It hasn't been for you," Jacobs said.

"It wasn't my success. I didn't get credit for putting it all together," Baker said. "Nor did I connect the pieces. That was all George Soper. Besides which, I'm a woman and I can make a difference for women and children in a way I could never make a difference in the world of typhoid. We needed Dr. Soper's sanitary engineering degree in that one, not my medical degree."

"What do you think will happen next?" Jacobs asked.

"Dr. Soper finds Mary and we end this chapter," Baker said, handing Jacobs a new slide.

"Do you think he will find her?" Jacobs asked.

"If she keeps cooking it's a matter of time. One of these days she will make a mistake and be visibly dangerous enough for more than just George Soper to be after her. Then she will be caught and, I'm sorry to say, severely punished," Baker's face had turned grim.

"Sorry to say?" Jacobs said.

"Mary is an innocent. She does not understand germ theory, Dr. Jacobs. She does not know how to protect the people she cooks for. She does however, understand that the operation Dr. Soper wants her to have is dangerous and she has justifiably refused it since she is aware that she might not live through it. The Department of Health has not found other employment for her so that she can support herself as they have for other carriers, I'm sorry to say," Baker said sadly. "This chapter will be over and Mary Mallon will pay a high price."

Chapter 54

Emergency

Mary fit the key in the lock of the one bedroom she shared with Hal in Alphabet City and opened the door calling for him as she entered. Hal had taken up her manager responsibilities when she had left, announcing that it was easier to mop the floors once in awhile than to move.

Lucky came bounding through the room jumping on her gleefully, "Down Lucky," she said, scrubbing his ears to let him know he was loved. She took off her coat and hung it in the tiny hall closet that made up the little entry way that protected her privacy in the living room from people standing in the hall.

"Hal, I'm home," she called again. "The job's nice and it pays well but I miss you and Lucky somethin' fierce, havin' only the one day and all."

There was no answer. Mary looked puzzled. She hurried into the living room. She had expected Hal to be home. She had told him the time she would get home. Because he liked to take advantage of "her availability," as he called it, it was his habit to be there when she arrived.

Hal was half sitting on the couch, his breath coming in strident gasps. He was unable to sit comfortably and equally unable to lie down. His skin was pale and greasy with sweat.

"Hal! What's wrong with ya'?" Mary gasped, fear flooding her so that her legs felt electric with the terror.

"Pain," he managed. He had never felt such pain. It crushed his chest, raced down his left arm and up his neck, into his teeth and his jaw. He could not breathe. He could not move. He knew he was dying and he was terrified.

"I'll fetch the doctor," Mary said, reaching into the closet for her coat. "How long have you been like this?"

"Hours," Hal managed, spacing his words between breaths. "…thought it was indigestion."

"It's not the…" Mary asked, speaking her worst fear.

"No, not typhoid," Hal reassured her, knowing what her fear would be. "I think it's me heart."

"Don't die on me Hal Breihof," Mary said between pursed lips. "I need ya'. I don't have many friends you know."

She looked at him with love in her eyes.

He smiled back grateful for the knowledge that if he was to die before she got back, he had seen that look and it had been meant for him.

Chapter 55

Woodlawn

The rain fell in a steady drizzle at Woodlawn Cemetery in the Bronx. Mary stood beside Hal's grave thinking that it was a pretty place and that Hal would have liked it – although he probably would have liked it better if he could have been stowed somewhere in his favorite bar where he could have enjoyed the jokes.

"Do ya' think he would have liked it here, Lucky?" she asked their dog, who sat next to her as she absently rubbed his ears. Lucky wagged his tail at the sound of his name, and Mary interpreted that as agreement.

"We're both goin' to miss him," she said, choking back tears. She could not remember when she had cried like this. She wasn't the crying type. It felt strange. "I don't know what's happenin' Lucky. I feel like Job. Every time I think I've found a solution somethin' new happens to pull the rug out from under me. You know I just keep on breathin' and eatin' because livin' has become a habit, a habit with no joy in it."

She turned away from Hal's grave and started back toward the road where a taxi waited for her. It had been a great expense to take a taxi all the way out of the city, but she had wanted to bring Lucky. She knew she wouldn't come again. Too many things were pulling at her now. She had no anchor in New York.

Chapter 56
Lucky

Mary handed Lucky's leash to Aggie who stood framed in the door of a row house in Flushing. She was standing beside a young man, with hair as red as hers, who had his arm around her shoulders.

"He's a good dog," Mary said, controlling the sadness in her voice. "I like him. Aside from you he was me only company in that damned hospital. He kept me sane if the truth be known. But I can't take him with me where I'm goin'. He deserves a nice home. Thank you for your generosity in takin' him, the both of ya'."

"You can have him back whenever you want, Mary," Aggie said, looking up at her new husband to see what he thought.

"Indeed," he nodded.

"Wouldn't be fair to him," Mary said, eliminating argument. She turned and walked away, deliberately choosing not to look back. Lucky, sat on the stoop whining. As Mary moved down the street, he jumped up and ran to the end of his leash, barking after her as if to call her back.

Mary squared her shoulders and tightened her face. She refused to look back. She refused to cry.

Chapter 57

Woodruffs Gap

Woodruffs Gap in Sussex County New Jersey was a place of mountains, lakes and streams where people could come to recover from whatever ailed them, away from the noise and bustle of the city.

The Woodruff's Gap Sanatorium overlooked a mid-size lake out on Lime Crest Road. It was picturesque in a rustic way with many individual cabins clustered around a central building where the patients gathered for meals and activities.

The Sanatorium was abuzz with the news from overseas. In this August of 1914 declarations of war had been made throughout Europe like falling dominos. It seemed that much of the month had been devoted to battles between the French, British and German troops in Togoland and South-West Africa. War was waging in central Europe as well, where the Serbian army was defending against invasion by the Austro-Hungarians. Sabers were rattling between Germany and Russia and the papers were filled with stories from the various fronts.

Since most of the kitchen help had emigrated from Ireland, the discussion of the war had become personal. England was mobilizing, and Ireland was joining forces with their traditional enemy.

Mary was standing at a large table peeling and slicing carrots for the evening dinner.

"Did ya' hear the news, Martha?" Dora asked her voice breathless with excitement.

Mary had not gotten used to her new name yet and did not respond.

"Martha?" Dora persisted. "Are ya' day dreamin'? Did ya' hear the news?"

"Sorry," Mary said, matching the young girl's excitement with her own. "What news?"

She was expecting another tirade about the Irish joining the English from Dora whose father had died in a mine explosion in Wales caused by the cheapness of the English owners and who felt strongly that Ireland should join the Germans.

"The typhoid broke out in E Section," Dora said, she seemed near to exploding. "They've got five cases. Dr. Zimmer thinks somethin' got into the water supply. They got some kind of a specialist comin' all the way from New York City to investigate."

"Good Lord. What's the world comin' to?" Mary said, her hands seeming to turn to stone, her knife frozen above the carrots. "An expert ya' say?"

"Indeed," Dora nodded. "Someone famous all the way from New Your City."

Chapter 58

Broadway Restaurant

The Broadway Restaurant, with its bright red booths and counters, located just north of Times Square, was usually busy during all three meal times and after the theaters let out. While the ambiance was close to zero, the food was good and reasonable and the turn over was quick.

George Soper sat in a booth drinking ice water and questioning Leroy Milford, the restaurant owner.

"Can you describe her to me?" Soper asked, once he had discovered that a cook had left the restaurant's employ within hours of Milford having been accused by a local doctor of being the source of a typhoid outbreak.

"Irish, tall, blond, heavy set, blue eyes, remarkably strong," Milford said his tone brisk and businesslike. "Kept to herself mostly although she was always pleasant and professional. She was a very good cook. I was sorry to lose her."

"Can you identify her from this photograph?" Soper asked.

Milford looked at the picture of Mary lying in a hospital bed on North Brother Island. "It's not a very good picture, but it might be her. Marie's hair was blond and this woman's hair looks brown. Marie wears glasses and she's quite heavy. I can't be sure."

"When did you say she left?" Soper asked, making notes in the lined book he kept for each outbreak. He was disappointed at Milford's reply but he agreed that the photograph was not a good likeness.

"She left immediately after that doctor came in here threatening to close us down. She was in the kitchen when he came in ranting and raving. She couldn't help but overhear him. He sounded like a crazy man. Swore we'd given typhoid to one of our regular customers. How the hell he had determined that it was us I never did find out. Anyway, when her shift was over she asked for her pay and I never saw her again," Milford said.

"Is it usual that cooks leave like that?" Soper asked.

"Unfortunately all too usual," Milford said.
"They're a high strung bunch, cooks are. They take offense easily. Get angry easily. And when they're as good as Marie, have no trouble finding other work. Has Marie got something to do with the typhoid? Did it really come from here?"

"As I said, several cases have been linked to this restaurant," Soper said. "We investigate every outbreak and search for things each patient has in common. We look to see if they use the same dairy, have eaten raw clams or oysters in season and if yes, establish where they purchased them. We ask if they have eaten in restaurants in the previous 21 days and if yes which restaurants. Your restaurant came up in the last ten cases. It's a fairly standard procedure for isolating the cause of a disease. What did you say she called herself?"

"Marie Bishof," Milford replied. "She came with excellent references in case you're wondering."

"Did you call them, the references?" Soper asked, remembering back to the beginning of his investigation of Mary when James Daniels of Mrs. Strikers had told him that his customers were not good at checking references and the verification of that information that he had found in Atlantic City.

"What for?" Milford responded. "If she hadn't been the cook she said she was I'd have known it the first night on the job and fired her. Cooks come and go. They're not like chefs. Chefs stay and build a reputation."

"Did she sign a contract with you, anything in writing?"

"Are you joking?" Milford laughed.

"Just hoping," Soper replied. "The woman I am looking for has a distinctive signature.

"Do you think she left because of that doctor coming here?" Milford asked.

"The woman I am looking for has left every place she has worked as soon as typhoid has broken out," Soper said.

"There's more than one?" Milford asked, his voice becoming strident with tension.

"Dozens," Soper replied. "You see I believe Marie Bishof to be an alias for Mary Mallon, Typhoid Mary."

"Sweet Jesus," Milford replied.

Chapter 59

Aliases

George Soper and Josephine Baker had met in Soper's office to review their information about Mary Mallon.

"She's traveling under another alias," Baker said, sorting through the reports.

"Martha Brown in Woodruffs Gap, Mary Edwards in Atlantic City, Marie Bishof in New York, and those are the ones we know about. Perhaps it's time to alert the public to the fact that she's around. If we publish an article maybe people will call us because they've seen, hired or worked with a tall, heavyset, blond, Irish cook," Soper said.

"Do you have any idea how many Irish blonds there are in New York, New Jersey and Connecticut?" Baker asked.

"Thousands," Soper said.

"Maybe tens of thousands," Baker replied. "I wonder why she stays in the New York area. We know she's worked in Maine, Massachusetts and New Jersey. She could go anywhere but she stays around here."

"Maybe because she knows how the system works here," Soper said.

"The system is broken for her. All the employment agencies are on the lookout for her. I can't imagine why she hasn't moved to an area where we can't find her," Baker mused. "Maybe one big move in a life time is enough."

"One big move?" Soper asked.

"From Ireland. Maybe that move was enough. Unless she's got family here, or maybe she's got family somewhere else and she wants them to be able to find her if they want to," Baker said.

"We can make up stories from here to heaven and back and never know," Soper said. "The point is that she does work around here, we are getting at least some reports about her, and I have a feeling we might be getting closer to catching her. I'm going to put that article in the paper and see what happens."

Chapter 60

Ice Cream Shoppe

In the late afternoon, at 58th and Broadway a newsboy hawked his wares, "Extry! Extry! Read all about it! Typhoid Mary cooking in New York Restaurant."

A man rushed up and bought a paper, hurrying toward the entrance to the subway, giving himself something to read on his way home.

In a nearby ice cream shop two women, in tailored suits that reached their ankles and showed their brightly polished high button shoes, sat at a table gossiping over hot fudge sundaes.

"It's getting so you don't dare go out any more, Myrtle," Adella remarked between bites.

"If the Broadway Restaurant would hire Typhoid Mary she could be cooking anywhere," Adella agreed. "Except here, of course, because they don't cook ice cream."

The two women laughed at their joke.

Behind them, Mary could be seen sitting at her own table. As the two women rocked with laughter, Mary stood up and left the shop her face a mask of controlled rage.

Chapter 61

Typhoid Mary

In the family kitchen, two children could be heard fighting at the kitchen table.

"You did not..." the girl screamed.

"I did too…" the boy yelled back.

"Did not!"

"Did too!"

"Be quiet!" If you don't stop fightin', Typhoid Mary's goin' to come and get ya'. Then you'll know grief," their mother said in exasperation.

The two children stopped fighting and stared wide-eyed at their mother.

Chapter 62

Sloane Lying-In Hospital

The telephone was ringing when George Soper, wearing his lab coat and carrying a stack of reports, hurried through the door to his office.

"Soper," he said, placing the receiver between his ear and shoulder as he put the pile of papers into his inbox.

"Dr Soper, Ed Cragin here," said the familiar voice on the other end of the phone.

"Dr. Cragin, good to hear from you," Soper replied, picturing the distinguished founder of the Sloane Lying-in Hospital, the largest and most successful maternity hospital in New York. "You still delivering babies?"

"Of course," Cragin replied before cutting directly to the chase. "Is there any other life for me?"

"What can I do for you Dr. Cragin?" Soper asked, guessing that Edwin Cragin wasn't making a social call.

"I called because I have a typhoid epidemic here at Sloan Lying-in. None of the mothers have contracted the disease, but I have 25 nurses who are infected and I can't find a cause," Cragin said, a hint of desperation in his voice.

"There is always a cause, Dr. Cragin," Soper responded. "Have you tested your food handlers?"

"We thought that with so many infected it might be more general than food handling, but the tests of our water supply have just come back negative. Can you come over?" Cragin asked.

"I'm on my way," Soper said hanging up the phone and reaching for his hat, coat and gloves before realizing he was still dressed in his lab coat. He removed the white coat, threw it on a chair, and shrugged into his camel hair as he moved quickly to the door that separated his office from his waiting area.

He called to his secretary as he passed through the waiting room, "I'm on my way uptown to the Sloane Lying-In Hospital where they're having a typhoid epidemic and they can't find a cause. Call Dr. Baker and tell her where I have gone. This is very much in her area of interest. She should join me there at her earliest convenience. Notify Doctors White and Jacobs to come along as well. Cancel all my appointments for today if you will and notify tomorrow's appointments that I may be tied up."

The Sloane Lying-in Hospital, the largest of New York's maternity hospitals dedicated to the safe delivery of children, resembled all such institutions. As Edwin Cragin and George Soper hurried through a labyrinth of scrupulously clean halls, Cragin filled in the details of the outbreak and what he had done to address it.

"We've tested everything we can think of. We cannot find the source of this infection," Cragin said. "We even took samples from the walls and floors."

"How many people are infected?" Soper asked.

"None of the patients, as I think I mentioned, but twenty-five of my nurses. Two of them are dying Dr. Soper. Two of them are dying and I don't know why," Cragin said, his voice cracking with despair.

They arrived at his office, and he gestured to Soper, "In here."

Cragin's office was spacious. It contained a large work space where he, Soper and six other staff members could spread out files for the investigation.

"To start with I'll need the files on each of your typhoid patients," Soper said as he removed his hat, gloves and coat. Fastidious as always, he put his gloves in his pocket and hung his coat and hat on the coat rack beside the door.

"Yes, we had assumed you would want to see them," Cragin said. "They're already pulled for you. Over here."

"We'll need to question them if you haven't done so already," Soper said, pulling back a chair at the head of the table, taking the seat and then picking up a sheet of paper to write on. "I'll make you a list of questions we need answered. I want timelines on all their activities so that we can see whether there is a common place where they might have had something to eat or drink outside this hospital; a common restaurant, a common dairy, a common bakery, butcher shop. Any consistent overlap, the incubation period is 21 days. You can start right away."

"I am, as you might imagine rather short staffed, but we'll do the best we can," Cragin replied.

"I'll bring my own staff in here to help, of course. Is it all right with you if we take over this part of your office?"

"I have set aside two offices in addition to this space, and I have spoken with the laboratory about making itself available to you," Cragin replied. "If you need more space we'll make it."

"I am most interested in looking at copies of your personnel files," Soper said, pulling one of the nurse files from the stack. "Let's start with anyone on your staff who handles food. My most pressing question is: Who cooks for the staff? Who prepares food for your staff that does not cook for your patients? In particular who handles the breads, salads or garnishes?"

There was a bustle at the door and Josephine Baker was ushered in

"Ah, there you are," Soper said. "Dr. Cragin have you met Dr. Sarah Josephine Baker, I believe she is making significant improvements in your mutual area of interest."

"Dr. Baker, I am always happy to see you," Cragin said, smiling at the petite woman. "I cannot express my excitement at the progress you have made in setting standards for and licensing of midwives. I can already see the difference in infant mortality."

Josephine Baker smiled. Recognition like this from one of New York's most prestigious obstetricians was music to her ears.

"Thank you Dr. Cragin," she said.

In the nurse's dining room Mary was setting a plate of hot food before one of the half dozen nurses who sat at the long table that stretched from one end of the room to the other. There were six other nurses eating at the table all of them crowded at one end. Mary put her apron between her hand and anything she handled. To anyone looking it seemed as if the apron served as a pot holder to keep the heat of the plate from burning her hands. What was less obvious, because it would take both thought and observation to notice it, was that she used her apron with cold food as well as with hot.

"There you are, dear," Mary said, her voice soft with concern. "My, you look exhausted. Is there anything I can do to help?"

"You've done more than your share, Mary," the nurse, whose name was Minna, replied. "We couldn't have got on without you."

In Edwin Cragin's office, Soper and Baker were sitting at the conference table with files piled around them.

"This cook, Mary Brown, the records indicate she arrived three months ago in mid-November," Soper said, his eye fixed on the paper in front of him.

"Yes," Cragin agreed, looking over Soper's shoulder.

"Would you describe her to me?"

"If memory serves me she's Irish, a large woman, blond, with startling blue eyes. She's notably strong," Cragin said, searching his memory banks. "For a time her strength was a conversation piece because we needed her help after one of our orderlies was injured."

As Cragin spoke Soper slowly rose to his feet. Baker looked at him knowingly.

"She's known to keep to herself, a good cook, competent. What is it?" Cragin asked.

"My God. Is she here now?" Soper asked, a tinge of excitement coloring his voice.

"I suppose so. I'd have to look at the schedule to be sure," Cragin replied.

"If she were here, where would she be at this time?" Soper asked.

"In the main kitchen," Cragin said, concern and puzzlement warring for dominance of his face. "Whatever is it, Dr. Soper?"

Soper looked at Baker and muttered under his breath, "She must have lost her mind, cooking in a maternity hospital."

"Who?" Cragin demanded.

"Mary Mallon," Soper replied. When Cragin didn't recognize the name he explained, "Typhoid Mary."

In the nurses' dining room Mary was still setting out food for the shift that was having lunch at the moment.

"Typhoid on top of everything else we do. What next?" Minna remarked to the table at large. "Thanks Mary."

"Maybe you should change your name, Mary," the nurse named Fannie joked. "Next thing you know they'll be calling you Typhoid Mary and testing your stool samples."

The nurses around the table laughed at the joke. They did not notice the stillness in Mary's body.

"Typhoid Mary," Minna said, her eyes twinkling with humor. "Now wouldn't that be something?"

"Well, who's to say these days?" Fannie said, catching her breath. "They sure as hell didn't run samples on every single person who works here as a qualification for employment."

"I'll just be gettin' the sauce," Mary said to no one in particular.

"That was funny, Fannie," Minna said, wiping her eyes, where the laughter had brought tears. "Typhoid Mary."

In the kitchen Mary passed through the swinging door. She crossed rapidly through the busy prep area, past the stoves and tables where the great pots of food stood ready to serve the hospital's population. Women who were eating for two were generally hungry, and the hospital kitchen served large healthy meals.

"Are you feeling all right, Mary?" Harriet, who was the hospital's chief cook and Mary's good friend asked, concern wrinkling her forehead.

"I just need to catch a breath," Mary replied. "Would you mind keepin' an eye on me nurses for five minutes, Harri?"

"But of course not," Harriet replied. It was unusual for Mary to take a break during a shift, and Harriet was more than willing to accommodate her if she felt that she needed to step out for a minute.

Mary reached the cloak room beside the back door. She pulled her wool coat from the rack, swung it around her shoulders, picked up her purse, smiled at Harriet and stepped out the door.

"Five minutes," she said just before closing the back door behind her.

Soper, Cragin and Baker entered the nurses' dining room quickly, a little breathless from the pace at which they had descended from Cragin's office.

"Have you seen the cook Mary Brown?" Soper asked.

"She was here a minute ago," Minna replied, looking up with great curiosity. It was unusual for Edwin Cragin to make an appearance in the nurses' dining room even though he was known to keep track of everything that went on in his hospital.

"Where did she go?" Soper asked his voice urgent and demanding.

"Into the kitchen most likely," Fannie replied. "What ever's wrong?"

Soper did not answer but turned and walked through the swinging door. Cragin and Baker followed closely.

Soper exploded into the kitchen, the swinging door banging loudly against the cabinets behind it. The seven people cooking and chopping looked up in alarm.

"Have you seen Mary Brown?" he demanded, finding no evidence of Mary in his quick survey of the people working in the area.

"She went out for a breath of fresh air," the stout, red faced Harriet replied, an edge of resentment at being talked to in that tone of voice in her kitchen coloring her voice.

"How long ago?" Soper demanded, looking for all intents and purposes as if he was at the start of a race.

"Not long," Harriet responded. She was just wondering how much she should say to this stranger when she noticed Edwin Cragin.

"She'll be back in five minutes," she added.

"Thank you, Harriet," Cragin said as he followed George Soper to the back door.

The loading dock door slammed shut behind Mary as she hurried along the ramp, down three steps and out onto the drive.

In the hallway that separated the back door from the loading area Soper and Cragin ran toward the loading dock.

Mary walked quickly across the area where delivery vans generally waited to unload their supplies. She was visibly hurrying while trying not to appear to rush. As she reached the sidewalk she looked back toward the dock. A shiver passed through her body and she thought someone must be walking on her grave. She reached forward and lifted the latch of the gate that separated her from the crowd on the sidewalk, pulled the gate open a crack and slipped through.

Soper stepped out onto the loading dock. Without hesitation, he ran across the dock, jumped down onto the drive, and raced across the cobblestones as the gate that gave entrance to the delivery area swung shut. He was too late. Beyond the gate was an empty space that lead to a busy thoroughfare filled with passing people. There was not a sign of Mary Mallon.

"She must have been very careful, Dr. Soper," Josephine Baker remarked when they had returned to Cragin's office and resumed their search through the Hospital employment records. "She was able to work here for three full months before infecting anyone. She must have taken extraordinary measures to protect the food."

"You can't be careful with Typhoid, Dr. Baker," Soper said. He was obviously working hard to control his rage and frustration. "You're either infectious or you're not and if you're infectious you don't handle food."

"It must be hard for her to understand, Dr. Soper," Baker said, keeping her voice calm and steady. "I don't believe she fully comprehends the concept of germs. But I do think that if she managed to keep from infecting the people here for three months that she understands dirty hands. I also believe that such precautions indicate that she is coming to some kind of realization that she is infectious."

"I don't care what she understands. That woman has infected twenty-five nurses in a maternity hospital, two of whom will probably not make it through the night," Soper raged. "I want her locked up and the key thrown away."

"With this degree of infection and irresponsibility, I would not be surprised if the government officials who were willing to allow her to leave North Brother Island might have a change of heart," Baker replied. "All we need is a little firm proof and I think you can get them to put out a warrant for her arrest if that is what you want to do. They might feel guilty enough to put out an all points bulletin."

"Look at this," Soper said, indicating an employment application and another document he had taken from a file that Baker had brought with her when she had joined him. "Here's Mary Mallon's signature on the release document she signed for the Commissioner of Health. Here's Mary Brown's signature on the Document of Employment she signed when she came to work here. Mary Mallon and Mary Brown both have exactly the same distinctive, well-rounded signature. I was that close to catching her, Dr. Baker. I missed her by seconds."

Chapter 63

Confession

Mary was blind to the beauty of the Church of Saint Paul the Apostle. She was not impressed by the massive gold dome above the altar, the famous murals and statuary or the magnificent stained glass windows. She made her way to the confessional like a man dying of thirst would move toward water in a desert.

"Forgive me father for I have sinned," she said, her voice choking with tears. "It has been eight years since my last confession."

"What are your sins, my child?" responded the anonymous voice on the other side of the screen.

"I have..." Mary began her rote response. She stopped herself. She felt as if she was dying with her life flashing before her. As she sat as still as stone, hardly breathing, she put the pieces together. Her eyebrows drew forward in a frown. She blinked rapidly, her head movements short and jerky as if she is looking for something. Her hand went to her throat as if the breath had been choked out of her. She looked up, pain visible in her eyes. "I..."

Her left hand brushed back an invisible strand of hair from her forehead. Her breathing became rapid with suppressed emotion, her chest heaved. Now her left hand pressed against her cheek moving back toward her temple. It wandered to her mouth to hide her trembling lips and her body began to rock in the agony of the moment. Tears stood in her bright blue eyes. Both hands now hid her face, sliding in an upward motion to become fists above her forehead.

An agonized shout issued from the confessional, "NO!"

The door crashed open. Mary, her hair disheveled, her face awash with tears, ran blindly toward the front door. Her right hand gripped her throat. Her left hand grasped the cloth across her chest. She ran up the aisle, bumping into several people as she escaped through the massive Cathedral doors.

On the stairs that led from the street Mary staggered and bumped into several more people.

"Watch where you're goin' lady," a heavy set man growled at her.

She did not hear him or slacken her pace.

On 59th Street Mary continued to run along the sidewalk, bumping, tripping, staggering, blinded by tears. People stepped out of her way as if avoiding a mad woman. She ran until she ran out of air. Then she turned into a blind alley where she sank down on her knees, put her head in her hands and sobbed for all the pain and loss of the past nine years.

Chapter 64

Arrested Again

The date on the *Daily Times* read, "March 27, 1915." The headlines were filled with news of the German blockade of England and the growing threat of the submarine attacks on commercial shipping. Everything had changed in this second year of the Great War. Fashion had taken an unexpected turn. Women no longer wore stays, because the metal was needed for bullets. Their clothing had been slimmed and reduced because material was needed for uniforms. Even though America itself was not yet in the war, the world's resources had been concentrated on the killing fields of Europe.

The people walking from the Flushing train station were mainly women. Among them was Mary carrying a large picnic hamper. Although she had taken to wearing eye glasses all the time and she had cut her long hair into a bob, she was easily recognized by her size and her manly stride.

Two men lounged against a wall outside the station. They were not wearing the uniforms of the police, but to the expert eye they would have been easily identified as members of the force.

Mary passed them, her eyes focused on the street ahead. She was having an inner conversation with herself about the possibility of changing her line of work from cooking to the factories. She had heard that the war effort had raised the salaries for women to livable levels and she was thinking that this might be a good time for a switch. It seemed that life for women was changing in America and she was definitely ready for change. She thought about Hal. He would have been too old for the draft, but he could have done well in the factories. How he would have enjoyed being paid a real wage.

The two men looked at each other knowingly. One pulled an artist rendering from his inside pocket and held it out where both could look at it. They looked at the picture. They looked again at Mary striding away from the station entrance. They looked at each other again, nodded and set off in pursuit.

Mary passed a group of row houses. There were picket fences around front yard gardens where spring flowers were pushing up through what was left of winter snow. Mary did not notice the grape hyacinths or the daffodils which at other times she would have admired. Focused as she was on the idea of leaving New York, she was oblivious to her surroundings. The food hamper swung in her hand, bumping unnoticed against her heavy thigh. Her thoughts were traveling along the lines of flight. She was worried about her narrow escape from the hospital. It had been madness to cook in such a place so close to George Soper. She had no reason to remain in New York. Perhaps she would go west. She had heard that Pennsylvania offered jobs, and Ohio. Maybe Chicago would be a good place to settle.

The two men followed her easily.

Mary opened the gate to Aggie's row house where she had dropped Lucky nearly four years earlier. Now she climbed the five steps to the stoop and knocked at the door. When the door opened there stood Aggie, her hand holding Lucky's collar, her face split in a welcoming grin. Lucky was bouncing and whining with excitement. Mary knelt down to fondle the shepherd so that he would stop pulling against Aggie's fragile arm. The dog calmed down and Mary entered the house. The door closed behind her.

Across the street, Detective Lincoln O'Shaughnessy said, "I'll telephone for reinforcements. If she goes anywhere else, follow her and call the station when you can."

Francis McAneny nodded and stepped back into the shadow of an alley. O'Shaughnessy walked back toward the train station toward a phone booth he had noted on the way in. McAneny rolled a cigarette. He leaned against a building smoking and watching. When he finished with one cigarette he dropped it and put it out with his foot, then rolled another one. Time was measured by the growing pile of butts at his feet.

The pile of cigarettes had reached to a dozen or more. McAneny still lolled against the brick wall of the alley when O'Shaughnessy rejoined him.

"They'll be here soon," O'Shaughnessy reported. "See anything?"

"All quiet," McAneny replied. "They didn't even walk the dog."

Around the corner a police wagon and an ambulance crept slowly to the junction and parked. Five uniformed officers stepped out. They moved casually to the alley where McAneny and O'Shaughnessy waited and joined them in the stakeout.

"You and you go around back," O'Shaughnessy said pointing to two of the officers who had just joined them. "Make certain she doesn't get out."

The two officers moved casually away from the alley, crossed the street and disappeared down a corresponding alley that would lead to the back of Aggie's row house.

"You three are back up," O'Shaughnessy ordered. "Don't move on her unless she resists."

The three officers acknowledged the order.

"She has a reputation for bein' very strong and very violent. Be prepared," O'Shaughnessy advised.

The three officers nodded, their faces pinched into expressions of extreme resolve.

"Let's go then," O'Shaughnessy said to McAneny who pushed himself away from the wall.

The two detectives and three uniformed officers crossed the street and approached the row house. They knew Mary Mallon by reputation and were already preparing to meet her aggression with aggression of their own.

O'Shaughnessy moved to the front door. McAneny and the uniformed escort fanned out behind him.

In Aggie's living room, Aggie and Mary were having tea and scones. Lucky lay with his black muzzle on Mary's foot as he had lain for so many years when it had just been the two of them.

"What will you do now?" Aggie asked, sipping her black tea with milk and sugar.

"I haven't figured it out yet," Mary said. "I was thinkin' of leavin'. Maybe goin' west where there's work in the factories that pays well, at least a great deal better than domestic service."

"What's keepin' ya'?" Aggie asked. Mary had been telling her about the typhoid epidemics and the close calls she'd experienced lately, particularly her escape from the hospital. She was afraid for her friend. "Now that ya' see that there might be a connection between you and the typhoid, wouldn't ya' be better off takin' a run at another line of work?"

"I would. But the last time I tried that it was a disaster and I don't have Hal to pick up the slack if things go bad for me," Mary replied, her face saddening at the memory of the ironing, her broken arm and the dying Hal. "There's not so many men like Hal in the world, ya' know."

"There's more for ya' to do now, you said so yourself," Aggie persisted, "more opportunity."

"I know. I can't stay here. I feel… ahhh, I don't know what I feel," Mary said fretfully. "I'm waitin' for an answer from God I suppose."

"These are good," Aggie said, helping herself to a cookie from Mary's hamper.

"Untouched by human hands," Mary retorted, "especially these human hands."

A heavy knock sounded at the front door and the two women froze with fear.

"Would ya' be expectin' someone, Aggie?" Mary asked, her apprehension standing clear in her face.

"No," Aggie replied with equal dread. "Now who do ya' think that could be?" She put down the tea cup and crossed to the window.

"You don't suppose God's messengers knock, do you?" Mary asked, her voice grim.

Aggie parted the curtain less than an inch and peeked out.

"Mother of God," she said, turning toward her friend with a look of total terror on her pale face. "It's the police, Mary. Go out the back."

"I don't think so," Mary said quietly. "Open the door Aggie. Hold Lucky and don't be afraid."

This time Mary went quietly. She rode sitting up in quiet dignity on the stretcher in the ambulance, staring out the back window, ignoring the detectives who sat on the bench opposite her.

Chapter 65

The Last Interview

    The isolation room in Willard Park Hospital for Infectious Disease looked exactly like the room in which Mary had spent the days following her first arrest. The room was small and predominantly white, only small squares of black in the white, germ-free linoleum floor. The bed was spare and white with white sheets and a white blanket. There were even white bars on the small single window. There was a small table with two chairs against one wall, and a wooden chair for company from which they could see the river.

    Mary, dressed in a white robe, was standing beside her window gazing out across the width of the East River with a deep longing in her eyes. There had been a perceptible change in the large woman, whose hair was now graying and whose blue eyes had lost their sparkle. She was no longer the angry spitfire who had been dragged kicking and screaming to her years of isolation nine years earlier. The fight seemed to have gone out of her. It had been replaced with a deep inner peace and dignity.

    When the key turned in the lock she did not bother to turn away from the window to see who was there. Nor did she show surprise when she heard the familiar voice.

    "Hello Mary," George Soper said as he entered her room.

    In the past Mary might have objected to his invasion of her privacy. Now she simply turned and said, "Ahhhh. If it isn't the pipe and drain man himself. Why, I might ask, am I not surprised to see ya'?"

    "It's been a long time," Soper said, noting the lack of fire in her eyes.

    "A life time, if the truth be known," Mary replied.

"They'll be coming to take you back to North Brother Island in a little while, but I asked to see you first," Soper explained, seating himself in one of the chairs by her little table. He placed his briefcase on the table, and opening it, removed a lined notebook and a pen. Next he closed the briefcase and set it on the floor beside his well polished shoes.

Mary turned back to the window. She had nothing to say to George Soper.

"There is so much I need to know about you, Mary Mallon," Soper began as if conducting the interview to which she had consented years earlier. "There are many important gaps in your life that need to be filled."

Mary turned and looked at him, studying his face. Her expression took on a growing amazement with each word he uttered.

"First we need to know exactly when you contracted typhoid?" he said, his pen poised to record her answer.

She did not move or utter a sound.

"How many outbreaks have you witnessed?" he persisted, as if she had simply been unable to answer his first question rather than choosing to remain silent. It seemed that he believed that by continuing with the questionnaire he would break down her will.

Mary stared at him, her face a completely blank mask.

"Where have you been these last five years?" he continued relentlessly. "Tell me Mary."

And then it happened. A slow smile spread over her face, a smile of complete understanding, a look which seemed to revitalize her, to bring her back to life.

"I won't tell ya'," she said with finality, pursing her lips shut as if to hold back everything he wanted to know.

"But it's important, Mary," Soper insisted. "Important to the world."

"No it's not important to the world," Mary said, her comprehension standing like a clarion call on her face and in her body language. "It's important to you. Without the information you're feelin' incomplete. And I'm goin' to let ya' stay that way."

Soper opened his mouth as if to argue, but she cut across him like a knife.

"You've been able to do with me whatever ya' wanted to do. You've taken samples of me most private parts against me will, deprived me of me livin', destroyed me good name, robbed me of a career I had spent a lifetime buildin', had me arrested, locked me away in solitary confinement for two years. Ya' nearly drove me mad, ya did. Now, you're goin' to lock me away for the rest of me life. The whole rest of me life in a prison on an island where no one else with typhoid has ever been kept."

Soper started to speak again. This time she held up her hand to stop him.

"There's no discussion here, *Mister* Soper. What ya' want to know is the last thing on earth that is truly mine and I will take it with me to the grave. Goodbye Mister Soper."

"Mary I..." Soper started to say. Then he stopped. He stood, put his pad and fountain pen back in his briefcase, turned toward her and gave her a small bow before letting himself out the door. "Goodbye Mary Mallon."

When he had gone, and the door had shut behind him, Mary turned to the window and stared once again across the river. She was resigned. Her life was over. There was no Hal to love her, no work to support her, nothing to keep her from vanishing onto that tiny island in the East River where she would die alone and forgotten.

She sighed heavily, tears catching in her throat as she stood and stared at life passing her by.

Epilogue

On North Brother Island Mary Mallon sat in the weakened sunlight on a wooden bench, surrounded by the barren tendrils of climbing roses in wintertime. She had turned her face toward the island of Manhattan, staring off into the distance to the place where the world was busy without her. A blanket was wrapped around her broad shoulders. She pulled it tight to keep out the damp cold of the river. A look of endless resignation marked her features. A photograph was taken on that day; a picture that depicted the great emptiness of the woman who had once had a fulfilling life as a sought after cook for the wealthy of the city.

Starting from her second arrest in 1915, Mary Mallon spent the rest of her life on North Brother Island. Although the New York Department of Health did not keep her in strict isolation any more, she was a virtual prisoner on the island. Over the years she made the best of the situation. She achieved the title of nurse for the other patients in the hospital – none of them typhoid carriers – and she learned to work in the hospital laboratory which brought her a degree of satisfaction. Although it was thought that there were hundreds if not thousands of typhoid carriers in New York City alone, and although Fred Moersch was said to have worked on the island voluntarily for a time, according to Emma Sherman who ran the Lab, Mary was the only typhoid carrier who was ever given a life sentence on North Brother Island.

Mary Mallon died, on November 11, 1938 at the age of 70 following a stroke which had left her completely incapacitated for six years. At the time of her death she had spent 26 years, more than a third of her life, as a virtual prisoner on North Brother Island. Eventually, even though she lived on the island, she was allowed to travel into the city for day visits to friends who still remained from her days of freedom.

Fifty-three cases and three deaths from typhoid were directly attributed to Mary Mallon, but because so little is known about her life before 1906, and because the Department of Health has been unable to piece together most of her activities during that five year period between 1910 and 1915, the true toll that can be attributed to her will never be known.

Contrary to the reports written by George Soper who claimed that Mary had never spoken about her plight, Mary wrote countless letters pleading her case to everyone she could think of. It was recognized that several carriers like Fred Moersch and Tony LaBelle were known to have infected and killed many more people through their handling of food than had Mary. It was also recognized that although Fred Moersch, like Mary, had gone back to cooking after he lost his job as a plumbers assistant and was discovered infecting his customers in a confectioner's shop, he was once again removed from food handling, but was never incarcerated.

In later years, Mary's hearing at the New York Supreme court raised many questions about the quality of her representation. The New York Department of Health did not have the legal right to incarcerate healthy carriers. Because Mary was the person who proved the theory that people who were apparently healthy could transfer disease, there were no laws dealing with healthy carriers on any of the books. Nonetheless, the Department of Health assumed such rights even though they were not actual law. George Francis O'Neill never questioned that assumption – which might have been the path to freedom for Mary. The absence of the legal right to quarantine healthy people was corrected several years later, well after Mary had been arrested, forcibly tested and kept in solitary confinement.

The New York Department of Health was known to arrange non-food handling jobs for typhoid carriers who were non-Irish, male, and married with families. Mary received no such help. Mary suffered from the effects of numerous biases. She was an unmarried woman, she was not attractive, she was Irish and she was a member of the servant class – all of which served to act against her in the decisions made by the New York Department of Health. One bias that is not mentioned in the literature about Mary, which may be the most compelling reason for her incarceration, is the fact that she cooked for the wealthy of New York. Had she cooked for the lower classes as Fred Moersch and Tony Labelle had done, it is probable that she might not have been singled out for a lifetime of punishment.

For her entire life Mary claimed that she was persecuted, and there is considerable evidence to prove that she was correct. Mary was a case of someone who did not have a voice in the world. Soper had the microphone and the ear of the press and no one allowed Mary to speak for herself.

The End

You have gotten to the end of this book so it must mean that you liked it. I appreciate that you've gotten this far. You know that as a self-published author it's really difficult for me to market my book the way that the big publishing houses do. So if you can take less than five minutes to write me a brief review, or choose the star rating to show how much you enjoyed it, I would really appreciate it. Here is the link to the review page on Amazon: http://www.amazon.com/dp/B004ZVD3BS. Once again, I greatly appreciate your helping me out and I want to thank you very much

If you enjoyed reading *Relentless: The Search for Typhoid Mary* you might also enjoy Joan Meijer's novel *The Provenance* – a medical drama which was inspired by the true story of an amazing rescue in New York City.

The Provenance
(Sample)

Chapter One

The Provenance, October 13th, 11:45 a.m.

A rendering of the building had been set in the corner of a plywood wall that separated the vast construction site from the city. Six feet tall and eight feet long, it showed a space age blue, block-square complex soaring forty stories into the background of a cloudless sunny sky. The building corners were rounded, the glass tinted so that it was impossible to tell where the building materials left off and the heavens began. Ground level featured dramatic setbacks and sculpted public gardens. The sign announced "THE PROVENANCE; site of the world's largest luxury condominium complex." The complex boasted a self-contained spa, Olympic-size pool, weight room, tanning salons, a parking garage and even an International Boutique Shopping Area for the "Perfect Vacation at Home."

The complex was a hole in the ground.

* * *

Supervisor's Office 11:45

Building Supervisor, Lou Zhornick, was a short, ruddy, bull of a man, with a curly pelt of salt and pepper hair that hugged his square head like a cap. He had a loud voice and immense energy. His surprisingly blue eyes snapped with intelligence and authority. He wore his leadership like an aura.

Zhornick had learned early that what people valued most about him was that he got the job done. No matter what it took, no matter what he had to do, he got the job done. That had been how he had survived as a kid and the pattern had stood him in good stead as an adult. His old fashioned father, determined to put spine in his brood, had strapped any kid in his large immigrant family who said, "I can't." Lou got strapped least of all.

"Get the job done," was Lou's First Rule Of Survival In The Construction Industry.

It had been his reputation for inspiring speed in his workers that had impressed the owners of The Provenance, the future behemoth high-rise project on Second Avenue. They had recruited him to be their new building supervisor. They needed someone to drive the project and he was their choice.

When they had brought Lou Zhornick on board, the project had been in the early stages of excavation. The owners had hit one snag after another. They were already three months behind schedule and several hundred thousand dollars over budget. Lou Zhornick was to be their savior. Within weeks he had begun to perform his miracles. He was under the gun and saying, "Get the job done!" louder than ever.

Among his men, Lou Zhornick had the nickname, "Shortcut." They loved him for it. It meant that no one was looking over their shoulders all the time. As long as they got the work done and it looked okay, it was good enough for Lou. There was something deeply satisfying about pure bull and jamming, even if customers sometimes complained that their kitchen cabinets fell off the walls, and that there were holes in closets big enough for cats to crawl into.

On Thursday, when half the rods for the reinforced concrete walls had come in short, he ignored the problem and installed the defective rods along one small section of the Second Avenue rim. It had gotten the job done, but had effectively weakened the structure. Lou had given it some thought before he made the decision. He did the math and figured that the only way the change in building plans would become evident was if tons of stress was placed against the outside of the weakened walls. There was actually only one segment of the foundation that was truly vulnerable, a short segment of wall where he had completely run out of the longer rods. It would have been better if he had noticed the shortage earlier, he thought, feeling his temper rise like blood pressure. That way he could have staggered the short rods throughout the wall instead of concentrating them in one place, but who had time to notice much of anything in the crisis that had become his responsibility.

Zhornick shrugged. What could possibly go wrong? Thank God architects always built redundancy into their plans. Redundancy took time and money and Lou Zhornick had leeway for neither. As he made his calculations he was secretly saying a little prayer of thanks to the Patron Saint of Redundancy.

Lou was good at praising speed and problem solving. He was murder when there were delays. He was not particular about rules being followed either. "Rules are made to be broken," was Lou Zhornick's Third Rule of Survival in the Construction Business, right after, "Have someone handy to pin the blame on if something goes wrong," which was his Second Rule. "There's thousands of rules being broken at thousands of sites around New York," he was fond of reminding his men. "So who's lookin'?" was one of his favorite questions.

A case in point had been his compliance with safety regulations regarding pedestrian access to sidewalks passing under heavy equipment. When it seemed he'd need three men to build a small fence, and he found he couldn't spare them, he ignored the regulation. The fence was supposed to block pedestrian traffic from the sidewalk between the excavation pit and the new building crane they had erected on Second Avenue late the previous afternoon. It could wait.

A delivery truck arrived. Lou needed the men to off-load supplies. He had his priorities straight – supplies were necessary, overtime was not. Protective plywood fences could wait. He could deal with the problem later. They could easily put up sawhorses to keep the damned pedestrians away. Lou muttered under his breath as he walked to his office trailer, "Stupid people, walking around construction sites, craning to see what was going on in a big, empty hole. If they wouldn't walk under a simple ladder for fear of bad luck, why would they walk under a 35-ton building crane hefting a half-ton of steel girders directly over their heads? Who was kidding who?" The phone rang and Lou forgot to order the sawhorses.

"Keep the men happy," was Sub-Section "A" of Rule Number One of the Lou Zhornick Code of Survival in the Construction Business. Lunchtime was important to the men on the shift and Lou always released his men on time for their break. The last thing he needed was union trouble on a job that was already substantially behind schedule.

Today he had a problem. The truck with framing girders came ten minutes before noon. Lou was royally pissed. He had a delivery man working on the clock and his crew was already at lunch. He tried to talk the driver into taking his lunch at noon with the men, but Eddie Bosche would have none of it. Bosche claimed he was behind schedule himself and needed his truck off-loaded before two. Lou looked around for Joe Zabiglione but the crane operator was nowhere to be found. Bill Arthur said Joe had left a few seconds earlier to take a leak before break. Lou felt the blood flood his face, why couldn't the son of a bitch take a piss on his own time?

"I guess he had to go," Bill Arthur said with a shrug.

* * *

Joe Zabiglione 11:45 a.m.

Joe Zabiglione never gave a second thought about his habit of leaving the keys in is rig. He always left his keys in his rig. If he had been asked why, which had never happened in the twenty years he'd been on the job, he would have replied, "Who the hell's gonna move a fuckin' 35-ton crane with 140-feet of steel boom attached to it?" He would then have taken off his hard hat and scratched his head, as was his custom when pretending to think. But someone did want to move his 35-ton building crane. Someone wanted to use his rig very much.

* * *

Earl 11:46 a.m.

Earl Latimore, tall, slender, handsome, with chocolate skin and large brown eyes, looked more like a college student than a day laborer. He had been hanging around looking for work for days. He had the feeling that if he could only hold out, if he could only manage to stay visible, this guy "Shortcut" Zhornick would give him work. He'd heard a lot about Lou Zhornick bending rules. He was waiting.

It seemed he'd been waiting for a break all his life. If Lou would bend one rule for him maybe afterward he could be made to circumvent the grandfather clauses that stood between Earl, licensing and a job that paid real money. Maybe he could get his chance. Shit, he'd do anything for a chance.

* * *

Lou Zhornick 11:46 a.m.

"Where's that black kid always askin' for work?" Lou Zhornick asked, looking at the pile of girders on the truck.

He spotted Earl leaning patiently against the south wall of his office.

"Hey kid! Yeah you. You wanna job 'a work?" Lou shouted.

"You kiddin', Man? Jus' you lead me to it," Earl grinned, his white teeth flashing in his handsome ebony face.

"If I remember correctly, you said you drive heavy equipment," Lou put a companionable hand on Earl's shoulder.

"Yes, suh," Earl responded eagerly. Lou liked the young man. He seemed eager and he was polite. Not uppity like some he'd seen on the jobs.

"Ever worked a crane before?"

"Yes, suh, Sea Bees," was Earl's quick response.

"Good. Move them girders from that truck to the floor by that wall over there. Do it before the regular driver gets back and I'll pay you double for the hour and give you somethin' steady." Lou spoke the magic words. He wasn't certain he meant them, getting the kid steady work could be more trouble than it was worth, but they sounded good and they had an immediate effect on the kid.

"Consider it done," Earl's grin spread from ear to ear. He looked at his watch. Before the end of the lunch hour wouldn't give him much time. He'd have to make the payloads pretty heavy to move all the girders in only one hour.

"Just get the job done!" Earl knew the First Rule in Lou Zhornick's Code of Survival in the Construction Business by heart. Because he knew the rule, he didn't mention the fact that he couldn't get a license. 'An',' he thought happily, 'the Man didn' ax.' Any other contractor would have been looking for paper. Paper was Earl Latimore's problem.

Everybody knew about the Catch 22 in New York, first you get the job, then you get the license. You can't get the job without the license and his Discharge stood like the Great Wall of China between Earl, licenses and construction jobs. If the Man knew all about Catch 22, and he didn't ask about the license, then the Man didn't want to know about anything except getting the job done. Today Earl would get the job done. Lou could help him hassle the licensing bureau later.

Joyously Earl sat himself in the driver's seat of the giant crane. The keys were in the ignition, Lou must have asked the regular driver to leave them. Earl's hands reached toward those keys as if they were the Holy Grail. He knew he was a good crane operator, the best. Now he had his chance to prove it. Skillfully he began the process of getting the job done.

* * *

Danielle 12:05

Danielle Danforth, her short brown hair ruffled by the slight breeze that funneled through the deep canyons between New York's tall buildings, had slowed her walk to a stroll. She couldn't resist the sun, even when pressured by the urgent need to return to the office while the terms of her last meeting were still fresh in her mind. Cat-like, she stretched her neck to let her face catch the last autumn rays. Soon enough it would be winter and she would have to pull herself in to conserve heat.

The promise of winter was all around her. The sun wasn't warm. There was a nip in the air that brought with it a feeling of gratitude for her down coat. She had elected to wear it when she left her brownstone earlier that morning. Her years of living against the weather in Vermont had trained her never to take weather for granted.

Danielle's mind jumped from the contract to a non sequitur. Maybe this year she'd go back to Aspen or Tahoe. The girls would like that after the ice, rocks and lift lines of the northeast. Her face softened as she visualized Brooke and Stacey's little faces laughing against the snow. To tell the truth, she'd like it too. She'd love it. She hadn't been out west since the winter before Mark died.

Strange, she had tried so hard to keep life the same since Mark had gone, but she had missed taking a trip west for skiing in powder. Perhaps thinking and planning a skiing vacation like this meant she was coming alive again. She hoped so.

She frowned slightly, the creases marring her otherwise perfect skin. Danielle was habitually hard on herself. Disciplined, organized, successful, she gave herself small margins for errant thoughts about winter vacations.

Ahead of her a giant crane squatted like a graceless Brontosaurus beside a sidewalk cluttered with pipes, culverts, beams and tubes; the assorted detritus of the building trade. Instinctively she slowed her pace.

"Never walk under a ladder," her mother's carping voice cautioned like a recording in her head.

"It's not a ladder, it's a crane," Danielle's mind argued back. Such a threatened woman, Fiona McCarthy, always predicting doom and gloom.

"It doesn't look safe to me," Fiona's querulous voice persisted. How the hell had her mother's voice taken such root in her head? Early childhood programming was such a bitch!

"If it wasn't safe someone would have blocked it off," Danielle settled the argument in her mind. Later she would wonder if she had chosen to walk under the crane because Fiona's voice had argued so strongly against it.

"A stitch in time saves..."

"Oh shut up!" Danielle forced the points she must include in her new contract proposal to the front of her mind. Early in her life she had discovered that she could only focus on one thing at a time, and that business was the great weapon for peace. Business always seemed to quiet Fiona's strident voice. Sometimes Danielle wondered if she was crazy. Fiona had been certifiable. Maybe insanity ran in the family.

* * *

Sylvia 12:05 p.m.

Ahead of Danielle, Sylvia Sabartini, her long braid of thick black hair swinging down her back, was humming her favorite few notes from Verdi's *La Traviata* as she strode under the crane. Grand Opera, she had discovered, was generally marvelous and occasionally sublime. Once in a while she found a few notes of a musical line that were so outstanding that she waited through an entire production to savor them. Those were the musical moments she went to hear. The way other sopranos performed her favorite moments was her measure of their talent.

Behind Sylvia, the crane lifted its heavy load of steel from the flat bed of a parked truck and slowly began a swing that would carry its awkward cargo across the sidewalk before lowering the thick, heavy girders into the excavation pit.

Sylvia's black eyes caught the shadow of steel passing over her head, as the bulk of the freight momentarily blocked the sun. Instinctively she quickened her pace. Much later she would say that the shadow, like the specter of a giant bird of prey converging on a rabbit, had been the warning of impending danger that had saved her life.

* * *

Jane 12:05 p.m.

Behind Danielle, Jane Ackerman pushed her thick glasses up the ridge of her nose as she stopped to watch the crane hoist its massive load and begin its swing across the sidewalk. How the hell could the crane lift so much steel at once, she wondered? It looked like an excessively large load, but what did she know?

In actuality, Jane had been fascinated by heavy equipment all her life and she knew a surprising amount about the business. She guessed that if she hadn't been a woman she might have tried to be a crane operator. Maybe it wasn't the fact that she was a woman that had kept her from pursuing heavy equipment. After all, she was an EMT, and when she'd started doing that women hadn't exactly been standing in line to staff ambulances. She tended to blame a lot of things she hadn't yet tried on the limitations of being a woman.

Jane firmly believed that she lived in a society that held a dichotomous view of womanpower. She was never sure whether it was the limits of society, or women's beliefs in the limits imposed by society, which kept them from successfully pursuing male-dominated work, but she supposed that didn't matter. In Jane's mind reality and perceived reality were much the same thing.

Jane was curious about the picture unfolding before her. Never before had she been able to see a crane actually work over a sidewalk. In the past the sight had been blocked off to pedestrian traffic by plywood barriers. It didn't register that her ability to see what was happening was due to a threatening lack of protection forgotten in the hurried morning schedule. She did not think to question the fact that the sidewalk was completely open to pedestrians. What she was watching was much too interesting for her to step aside and contemplate how unusual it was for her to be able to see it.

With rapt attention, step by curious step, she was drawn closer to the edge of the excavation. Each step gave her a better view of the intricacies of the process of crane operation. She was mesmerized by the way the driver used his dark hands on the levers. He was a master. It was almost like watching a ballet.

* * *

NYC Ambulance 474 12:05 p.m.

Laurie Higgins pulled the unit up to a fire hydrant space near the corner of 86th and Lexington. William Russo hopped out and ran to the corner deli. He cut to the head of the line and bought a ham on rye – heavy on the mustard, and a tuna on Wonder Bread – lots of mayo. He added a Power Bar, a Twinkie and two cups of coffee, one black, the other with lots of cream and four sugars.

"How can you eat that shit?" he asked, handing Laurie the Tuna, the Twinkie and the sweet, creamy coffee.

"I like scraping congealed bread off the roof of my mouth," she retorted, her mouth already filled with the creamy goo.

William shook his head and smiled. They had this same conversation almost every day. Her capacity to eat disgusting tuna sandwiches and Twinkies were two of the things William most loved about Laurie.

He opened his bit of health, began to push the food into his mouth and waited for the next call to come over the radio. Ambulance personnel learned to eat fast and whenever they got the chance. They lived with interrupted meals and indigestion.

* * *

Emergency Department Bellevue Hospital 12:05 p.m.

As Michael Rothman, M.D. stitched a lacerated finger in the surgery cubicle, he mentally grumbled about the fact that little lacerations were a terrible waste of his surgical talents. When he had selected surgery as a specialty, he had thought that every waking moment would be an adrenaline rush. He had never expected to spend most of his life battling drudgery. He was addicted to adrenaline and found himself wishing that something thrilling would come in over the radio so that he could stop making busy work and really be useful. He was bored and restless and wanted some action.

As he finished placing the last of the stitches in the laceration, he looked around to see which of the nurses was around. If he couldn't have action of one kind maybe he'd get action of another.

* * *

Earl 12:05

Happiness was a palpable aura radiating around Earl as he worked the controls of the giant crane. He whistled under his breath. After this they'd have to give him his license and a job. If he had a real job that paid real money he and Tamara could get married. The man had said he'd get work if he moved those girders. Doing an impossible job for a man who respected achieving the impossible above all else would overcome everything that had stood in his way for so long. The man had no curiosity at all beyond getting the job done.

Earl's mouth pulled into a scowl as his memories stole the happiness from the moment. All that Dishonorable Discharge stuff had been unfair anyway. Sometimes he felt as if God had it in for him. Shit, all he'd ever wanted was a chance to prove how good he was. Well here it was at last, a lucky break.

Earl pulled the levers to lift the load of girders and felt the crane respond sluggishly to his touch. He knew he was seriously overloaded, but what the hell, he had a deadline to meet.

Deadlines to meet and jobs to be got, it sounded like a poem, maybe a poem by Robert Frost; Robert Frost Latimore. Maybe he'd name his first son Robert. Nice name. Or maybe he'd name him Work. Work. A fine name. That was the name of life's game. He'd teach him early. His bitter sister was dead wrong, damn her. He would get out of the Ghetto.

* * *

Second Avenue 12:05 p.m.

Six feet below the sidewalk a water main that had been installed near the turn of the century, felt the weight of the crane pushing against its sides. The main had been eroded over the years, its tensile strength reduced to a thread by the persistent washing against it. For the moment it held. But here and there microscopic cracks appeared in the smooth metal surface, a promise of damage to come.

* * *

Lou 12:06 p.m.

Lou Zhornick had spent the past half hour on the phone. Son of a bitching Unions always came up with their demands when he had tight deadlines to meet. The thought had him in a rage. Somebody from the job must have called them. The fuckers knew he was behind schedule, knew he was between a rock and a hard place, knew that this was the time to push for concessions.

Lou had become so involved with his new crisis that he had forgotten about the crane working illegally over the unprotected sidewalk high above him. He had a nagging feeling there was something he'd forgotten, something important he should have done, but he couldn't for the life of him remember what it was. All he could think about was the major work stoppage that loomed on the horizon. To meet the goals he had been hired to achieve he simply could not afford to lose one damned hour from his work schedule.

* * *

Provenance Excavation 12:07 p.m.

The crane swung its load across the sidewalk and began lowering the mass of girders toward the bottom of the excavation site. The weight of the boom and the heavy material it carried rested fully on the wheels and bracing feet closest to the excavation pit.

Below those bracing feet, microscopic cracks appeared in the sidewalk. Near the excavation pit, compressed earth began to bulge with the weight of the overload. The areas of weakness just above the concrete wall, which had not been reinforced because of those short rods, delivered erroneously to the site weeks before, began to displace outward.

Just as Lou Zhornick could not conceive of losing one hour from his work schedule, so had Lou Zhornick been unable to conceive that 35-tons of lateral pressure would ever be exerted against the walls of his excavation pit before cross beam support had been installed to offset the below-standard workmanship. Now the things that Lou Zhornick had been unable to imagine were about to become his reality.

With a sound like a cannon shot, the walls burst and a seam of compressed earth spewed from behind the cement just below the feet of the crane. The sound of disaster, like a cannon in a small room, was followed by an intense silence. In the distance it was possible to hear the background noise of traffic, wheels on tarmac, impatient horns. At the building site it was as still as a forest, as calm as the sea before a storm.

Everyone who heard the sound searched for its source and found nothing immediately threatening. An eternity of minutes later, groaning like a wounded prehistoric animal, the crane slowly began to tilt over onto its side. It started in slow motion and gathered speed as gravity exercised its inevitable pull on the unbalanced behemoth.

* * *

<u>Inside the Excavation Pit 12:07 p.m.</u>

When the wall let go, the boom of the crane was almost at its off-loading point. Weighted by its load, and because of its position deep in the excavation pit, the boom hit bottom before the crane body came to rest on the pavement high above. For endless seconds the top of the boom drove into the cement floor. Metal on concrete screamed like a thousand fingernails dragging across a blackboard. The fingernail sound was quickly replaced by a deeply pitched scream as the 35-ton monster adjusted to the sudden stop through all its myriad joints and connections.

It had been a miracle that the boom had not slid out from under itself in the vastness of the pit. If it had not landed point first, and imbedded itself deeply into the concrete floor, nothing would have prevented the crane from toppling the rest of the way into the pit. If the boom had let go there was nothing to stop it from sliding all the way to the far wall of the block-square hole. Without the support of the boom, the body of the crane would tumble the rest of the way into the pit taking the remains of the sidewalk with it. Earl Latimore would certainly have been crushed as the crane landed cab first on the cement pad 30 feet below street level. Danielle Danforth, Jane Ackerman and Sylvia Sabartini would have been spilled into the depths of the pit to face varying degrees of injury or painful death. Four lives depended on a trembling arm of steel buried six inches deep into the floor of the future building.

For a moment, its momentum halted, the boom bowed with tension, threatening to shake itself out of its sudden stop. There was utter silence in the pit as the boom quivered with unspent energy.

Like the motions of a burrowing animal, the quivering followed the fault lines in the cement, driving the top of the boom deeper into the reinforced concrete until its energy had been spent and it finally came to rest standing awkwardly on its rigid neck. Welded together, the boom and the cement floor were all that stood between Danielle, Earl, Jane, Sylvia and total disaster.

* * *

Danielle 12:07 p.m.

Danielle's first awareness of impending disaster was auditory. She could not identify the source of the cannon shot, but she could hear the earth moving before she felt the sidewalk heave beneath her feet. Instinctively she ran forward, her athlete's body carrying her away from the perceived source of danger.

Her quick move saved her life. Seconds after she dove toward safety, the thick base end of the boom slammed into the sidewalk where she had been walking. But, even with those quick reflexes, her actions were not enough. As the sidewalk bucked and danced beneath her feet, Danielle tripped, sprawling under the body of the toppling crane. The slope of the sidewalk flipped her up and around, throwing her back under the cab and twisting her body so that her head now pointed in the direction of the pit.

As more dirt was pushed from beneath the sagging sidewalk, by the weight of the settling crane, Danielle started to slide headfirst into the thirty-foot drop just beyond her head. The terror of her scream was lost in the far greater noise of the boom connecting with the floor of the excavation pit and the sound of tearing steel as the crane settled into its own weight.

Danielle was unaware that the buckling sidewalk, which was creating her inexorable slide toward the thirty-foot drop, had saved her from a new peril. With only inches to spare, her slender body slipped out from under the massive wheels that threatened to crush her chest, her abdomen, and her hips. She might be dropped on her head, but she would not be crushed.

The nails in Danielle's desperate fingers tore to the quick as they sought purchase in the bucking cement, but she felt no pain. Neither did she feel pain when the sheet metal that comprised the crane's giant fenders, the most prominent part of its anatomy, grabbed her across her thighs, pinning her to the sidewalk, stopping her downward plunge, and simultaneously crushing the large bones in each of her thighs into multiple fragments.

At precisely that moment, the boom dug into the floor of the pit. This quivering, tentative halt stopped the full weight of the crane from spontaneously amputating Danielle's legs above the knees. Now she lay on the rim of the pit, head slightly down, safe, hurt and fully trapped by 35-tons of unstable metal.

The sidewalk, mutilated by millions of cracks in every direction around her, was holding by dint of a few pieces of wood and a minor miracle that no one in the city or building crew had been aware existed. The wood, the vestige of support scaffolding, had been scheduled to be removed when the next stage of building was undertaken. It was a matter of timing that had kept it in the right place to prevent Danielle's final tumble into the pit. The unknown miracle was that thirty years earlier, a frustrated owner-contractor, in an effort to prevent frost heaves, and limit his recurring maintenance problems, had laid a tough layer of steel netting into the new concrete he was pouring to replace the sidewalk in front of his building. The steel netting, resting against the remains of scaffolding, now held the sidewalk in one piece, preventing it from splintering into bits and dropping Danielle into the pit.

At the moment, Danielle was unaware of the miracle. As the bones in her thighs fractured under the weight of the fenders, she lost consciousness. She was in another time, another place. Another world.

About Joan Meijer

Joan Meijer started her writing career as the co-author of the last five Suzy Prudden books, including: *MetaFitness: Your Thoughts Taking Shape, Change Your Mind Change Your Body, Starting Right, Suzy Prudden's Itty Bitty Weight Loss Book, Suzy Prudden's One Stop Diet Revolution* and *Suzy Prudden's Body Mind Connection*. She has written five fiction and non-fiction books under her own name including *Date Rape: It's Not Your Fault* and *The Provenance, How To Write A Book That Positions You As A Leader In Your Field* and *The Character Book: How to Develop Characters for Writer, Actors and Readers of Fiction*. She also writes medical thrillers under the pen name John Russell, including: *The Initiative* and *The President's Dirty Little Secret, Accidental Consequences* and the soon to be released, *15 Seconds: A Cautionary Tale of What Might Happen If America Continues To Ignore Its Infrastructure*.

CPSIA information can be obtained
at www.ICGtesting.com
Printed in the USA
LVHW011621250520
656560LV00011B/706